"Don't ever expect me to try and seduce ~~you~~ **said, yanki** ~~ng~~ **stall door**

Ken stood frozen ~~as the water went running~~ down his perfect ~~back. "Never learn how to~~ knock?" he asked, his voice a low, husky drawl.

Pamela's tirade ended as her breath exited her lungs. "Oh, my," she whispered, unable to look away. She had already seen his beautiful bare torso and flat stomach so rippled with muscles, but now she saw the rest of him—the lean hips, the long legs and, oh, the *rest* of him.

Pam began to shiver. "I want you, Ken McBain," she said, tugging off her T-shirt and tossing it to the floor. "But your nobility is killing me. So take me or leave me."

He'd been able to hold firm before. But there was no way he could resist her now, the burning look in her eyes, the anguished need in her voice.

He nodded toward a basketful of condoms on the bathroom counter. "Grab a handful of those, would you?"

Dear Reader,

What could be more irresistible to a woman than coming across a gorgeous single man whose eyes tell her how much he wants her? That's the dilemma facing Pamela Bradford on what should have been the worst night of her life. A bride without a groom, a woman who's spent her entire life denying her sensual nature, she's now ready to indulge in her wildest fantasies. And sexy Ken McBain is just the man with whom she'd like to indulge.

Ken, however, just wants to look after Pamela. Sure, his libido kicks into high gear every time he's around her, but as far as he's concerned, there's going to be *no sex!*

It's going to take some serious convincing—in a resort that promises to "wash away every inhibition"—for Pamela to change his mind. Let's just say she's *relentless* in her pursuit.

This is my first Temptation HEAT novel, and I've had a lot of fun writing it. Where else could I have come up with a setting like The Little Love Nest—a resort with round beds, mirrored ceilings, suggestive statuary and a hostess named Madame Mona. I think I like pushing the envelope. I might just have to try it again.

I'd love to hear what you think of Pamela and Ken's amorous adventures. You can write to me at P.O. Box 410787, Melbourne, FL 32941-0787, or e-mail me through my Web site—www.lesliekelly.com.

Enjoy,

Leslie Kelly

Books by Leslie Kelly

HARLEQUIN TEMPTATION
747—NIGHT WHISPERS
810—SUITE SEDUCTION

RELENTLESS
Leslie Kelly

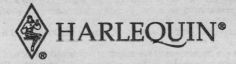

HARLEQUIN®

TORONTO • NEW YORK • LONDON
AMSTERDAM • PARIS • SYDNEY • HAMBURG
STOCKHOLM • ATHENS • TOKYO • MILAN • MADRID
PRAGUE • WARSAW • BUDAPEST • AUCKLAND

Dedicated with love to Ray Smith....
Dad, thanks from the bottom of my heart
for always encouraging me to be a dreamer.

ISBN 0-373-25941-7

RELENTLESS

1

SUFFOCATING BENEATH ten pounds of buttercream icing in a paper, cardboard and wood-framed tomb, Pamela Bradford noticed immediately when her whiskey sour buzz wore off. Her mind suddenly cleared, her stomach began rolling around and her hands started to shake.

"Get me the heck out of here," she ordered in a loud whisper, not even knowing if any of her bridesmaids were still nearby. A giggle and a muttered "hush" told her they were. "Sue? Sue, I've changed my mind. I can't do it."

"Yes, you can," someone replied.

That wasn't the voice of Sue, her sweet-natured maid of honor, who was timid as a rabbit about everything except her passion for romance novels. No, the voice sounded cynical but amused, gravely and authoritative, as only the voice of a strong, confident, two-hundred pound African American woman could.

"LaVyrle, please, this was a bad idea. Peter's not going to be very happy about this."

"Not happy? Girlfriend, puh-lease! That man's going to bust into a raging ball of male heat when he sees you come outta this cake. And if he doesn't, well, at least you'll know tonight, rather than tomorrow after you marry the pansy. Now be quiet, we're still working on our evacuation plan."

Pamela sighed, knowing LaVyrle would not take pity on her. Sue, yes. Pamela's best friend Sue, who'd been a perfect little angel as a child—except, of course, when Pamela was around—would have let her out in a heartbeat. But not with LaVyrle and Wanda in the room. She'd be no match for Pamela's two friends and co-workers from the teen center in downtown Miami.

Since Pamela had once seen LaVyrle physically tackle and take down a street dealer who'd approached some of their boys leaving basketball practice, she didn't think she _wanted_ Sue to try standing up to her.

She could burst out of the cake now, she supposed, avoiding the bachelor party altogether. But since her friends had pushed her into a hallway of the Fort Lauderdale hotel, she figured that wasn't such a great idea. With her luck, she'd run smack dab into the local gossip columnist or a vacationing family with six young kids, complete with Mickey Mouse caps, big eyes and a camera!

"Good grief," Pamela muttered, knowing she was stuck, in more ways than one.

Folded in half, with her knees tucked under her chin, she couldn't move an arm to scratch an itch without risking a heaping headful of icing. She glanced up, seeing that the top of the paper cake, just inches above her eyes, was lower than before. The wooden frame wasn't dealing well with the weight of the gooey icing. "I didn't think they put real icing on these stupid things,"

Pamela said and glared at the frame, hoping like hell it would hold up a few minutes longer.

"They don't, usually," LaVyrle said. "The best man, or whoever the dude was who hired my friend Nona to strip tonight, paid extra for the icing. Some guys do that, you know. Then the birthday boy—or the groom—has to lick the stuff off the dancer."

Pamela swallowed hard.

"Of course, we all know Peter wouldn't do that," Sue chimed in. Thank heaven for sweetly optimistic Sue.

"Well, he'd sure better now," Wanda retorted. "Pamela, I bet Peter's gonna want to lick off every speck. Unless he don't like girls...uh...I mean, sweets!"

Pamela's stomach rolled again. "Please let me out."

"You just have cold feet. Quit whining!" LaVyrle ordered.

"I have a cold butt is what I have," Pamela muttered. Her friend's low chuckle told her she'd heard. Pamela shifted a little and wondered how she'd gotten into this mess.

Though she couldn't move her head too well, she did cast a quick glance down at herself, and shuddered. Yes, she still wore the ruby-red, glittery pasties and matching thong, plus the spiked high heels LaVyrle called "do-me shoes."

Okay, so she had a top on over the getup. But the filmy, nearly sheer shirt fell only to her thighs. It was also so thin it offered no protection for her nearly naked backside seated directly on the cold metal shelf of the pushcart.

This was one heck of a way to spend the night before

her wedding. She still couldn't believe she'd agreed to
it. What had she been thinking?

Well, actually, she knew what she'd been thinking.
She'd been listening to that teeny tiny voice in her brain
that had been nagging at her lately, asking why Peter
hadn't tried to move their relationship from emotionally intimate to physically intimate.

Her fiancé hadn't so much as attempted a single
grope in the entire six months of their relationship!
He'd kissed her, yes, sweetly gentle kisses that hinted at
a restrained passion. But nothing more.

So why are you marrying him? she asked herself in a
rare moment of pessimism brought on by whiskey
sours and itchy spangled underclothes.

She didn't have to search for an answer; she knew
why. Peter might not have seduced her physically, but
he had bowled her over emotionally. She'd never met
another man with whom she was so perfectly in sync.
They shared the same tastes in everything—from sports
teams and ice cream to rock groups and political affili-
ations. They'd never had a single argument, never exchanged a cross word. Given Pamela's battles with her
parents, she found Peter to be a soothing presence in
her world.

It went even deeper than that. Peter was also the first
man she'd dated who completely and without reserva-
tion supported and applauded her career decisions. He
encouraged her to keep fighting for the underprivi-
leged teens she felt so passionately about. He consoled
her when she cried in frustration at her parents' contin-
uing refusal to accept the choices she'd made in her

life—choices that didn't include their country clubs, golf dates or yachting trips.

In their minds, she was merely going through a stage, or intentionally being difficult as she had been when she was a child. Okay, so she'd been a tough little cookie as a kid. She'd performed operations on her stuffed animals on the kitchen table, and used green and brown markers to draw camouflage outfits on all her Barbie dolls. She'd dreamed of making the basketball team rather than being a cheerleader. Not out of a desire to be difficult, but because she'd been born with a need to be true to herself—which meant being different from those who loved her!

Peter had supported that. He'd appealed to her brain, seducing her completely with his unwavering support.

But as for her body.... Had there been touches? Heated caresses? Seductive whispers or downright horny grins? Nothing. Nada. Zip. Zero. Zilch.

Pamela wasn't a sexual connoisseur—far, *far* from it!—but she had enough experience to know that people who were supposed to be in love enough to marry one another usually had some physical desire going on, too. Yet Peter had never made one serious effort to make love to her, even though she'd hinted that she wanted him to.

She'd heard about his reputation as a ladies' man. She'd been around her father's offices enough to know that Peter had had more than his share of female companionship—though, of course, that was all in the past. That fact made his disinterest in pursuing a physical relationship with her even more disturbing.

She'd gone so far as to plan the most romantic, enticing honeymoon she could think of! Egged on by one of those seductive ads in the back of a bridal magazine, she'd paid a small fortune to book them a room at a new honeymoon resort at Lake Tahoe. Peter thought they were going to a friend's lakefront cabin, and Pamela wasn't too sure how he might react to her surprise when they arrived at the luxury resort that promised to "wash away the outside world...and every inhibition." What if he hated it? What if he wanted to leave?

She shouldn't be having these fears about the man she was going to marry. They bothered her. More than bothered, they concerned, even *angered* her. So much so that, tonight, at her own bachelorette party, she'd allowed too much alcohol to loosen her tongue and had spilled her secret to her bridesmaids.

Sue's eyes had widened. Wanda had given her a look of outright skepticism. And LaVyrle had shrieked, "He's gay! I'm tellin' you, girl, you're about to marry a man who hangs out in steam rooms and goes to Bette Midler concerts!"

"He's not gay," Pamela muttered inside the cake. She knew Peter was straight, particularly given his love 'em and leave 'em history, yet she was unable to come up with a more logical explanation for her fiancé's physical disinterest in her.

One thing was sure. She could not be married to a man who had no interest in sex. Love was wonderful and she felt sure...pretty doggone sure, anyway...that she loved Peter. What wasn't to love? What woman wouldn't want to be married to a handsome, successful man who anticipated her every need, agreed with her every thought?

"Maybe a woman who needed some passion in her life," she muttered. Pamela simply could not imagine a marriage without desire. Not after seeing the passionate love her parents had for each other, still, after thirty years of marriage.

"My parents," she said with a grimace. If they could see their little princess/pumpkin/pookie-face Pamela now, they'd both be clutching their hearts, leaning against their matching red Beamers in horror.

"Okay, honey, we've got us a plan," LaVyrle said from somewhere above and to the right of Pamela's cakey coffin. "Sue's going to go in and tell Peter she has to talk to him about a last-minute wedding problem. While they're talking, Wanda and I are gonna bust in and say there's a bomb and everybody has to get outside. Only Sue'll hold Peter back."

"That's the stupidest idea I have ever heard," Pamela yelled. "Don't you think Peter's going to wonder why Sue wants him to stay and risk blowing up if there's a bomb?"

"She'll tell him you're the bomb, sweet cheeks! Besides, you got any better ideas?"

Pamela blew at a wisp of brown hair that had slipped from the loose mass of curls at her nape to fall over one eye. "Why not just tell the groomsmen there's a wet T-shirt contest in the bar?" Beneath her breath, she added, "Peter probably wouldn't be interested anyway."

"Yeah, Peter probably wouldn't be interested in that, anyway," LaVyrle said with a snorty chuckle.

Pamela muttered an obscenity.

"I guess it'll do. You just sit tight—don't you go any-where now." The other woman snickered again. "We'll go find out where the bar is and then come up to the suite to get the other men out. Back in ten or fifteen minutes to getcha."

"Please, LaVyrle," Pamela pleaded, "make sure you get every other man out of there. This is humiliating enough—the possibility that anyone other than Peter could be there to see me come out of this cake is too hor-rible to think about."

Particularly since most of the men at the party were Peter's coworkers—which meant they also worked for Pamela's father! The image of all of her father's navy-blue-suit-and-tie-wearing middle managers seeing her in the pasties and thong was beyond bearable.

"Back soon, Pammy," she heard Sue whisper. "It'll be okay." She listened as the three women walked away, their giggles lingering after them. That left Pa-mela alone in the small alcove near the hotel suite where the bachelor party was taking place. They'd moved her here after helping her get into the giant cake, which had been prepared for LaVyrle's stripper friend, Nona.

What an oddly bad coincidence that LaVyrle had happened to know the woman who was performing at Peter's bachelor party tonight. What a worse one that Pamela had chosen tonight to overdo it with the spiked punch. She'd been tipsy enough to spill her guts about her concerns regarding her potential sex life with her future husband. Her three friends hadn't let up once

LaVyrle had gotten the idea for Pamela to switch places with the stripper.

And now look where she found herself. Mostly naked. Inside a paper cake covered in icing so sweet the smell was making her nauseous. Curled so tight her legs were probably going to fall asleep and give out before she could pop out of the cake like a deranged, spangled jack-in-the-box. Unable to stop shaking as she waited to see either a wonderful look of lust or a horrible grimace of disdain on the face of her groom.

Why, oh, why had she agreed to do this?

As she had explained the time she'd broken her arm trying to see if she could fly by leaping off the roof of her parents' garage, Pamela muttered, "I guess it just seemed like a good idea at the time."

KEN MCBAIN sat in a back corner of the opulent hotel suite, alone, nursing a beer and asking himself for the tenth time why on earth he'd ever bothered coming to this bachelor party. He didn't know the groomsmen. He barely knew any of the men attending the party, their conservative, clean-shaven faces wearing similar goofy expressions that said, "Let's do something real dangerous like watch a dirty movie on the Playboy Channel." And to top it all off, he didn't even like the groom!

All in all, it was proving to be a wasted Friday night. Though he'd only been at the suite for about an hour, Ken was more than ready to leave.

"Pete, you remember these ladies, I'm sure," a man Ken recognized from the personnel department of Bradford Investments said as he entered the room. Behind him were two women—two very blond, very stacked, very professional-looking women, their profession being the world's oldest, that is.

The partying junior executives exchanged nervous glances and more nervous grins. Their eyes widened as Ken's rolled in amused disgust.

"Now this party's gonna roll," the groom said, lifting a beer—imported, of course—to his lips and chugging it. Well, he tried to chug it. He drained about half of the green bottle before pulling it from his lips and sucking in a deep breath.

The entrance of the party girls was Ken's cue to cut the hell out. He'd never had to pay for sex in his life and had absolutely no interest in being around guys who did.

He stood, preparing to do just that. Two of the other men—ones Ken had dealt well with in the few weeks he'd been working on the Bradford project—did the same thing. His respect for them went up a notch. As the groom grabbed the hip of one of the passing blondes, Ken's respect for him—already pretty damn low—dropped to toilet bowl range.

He couldn't believe Pamela Bradford—the Pamela Bradford whose smiling face had captivated him from the moment he'd seen her photo on her father's desk at their first meeting—was going to marry this womanizing loser.

Peter Weiss must have one amazing acting ability to go along with the *GQ* looks and oozy charm. Because, as far as Ken could tell from his single encounter with Ms. Bradford, she could have just about any man she wanted with the crook of a finger. Ken grudgingly conceded he had to include himself in that estimation.

And she'd chosen Peter. So either she was stupid and gullible, which he doubted, or Peter had snowed her about what he was really like. That seemed almost inconceivable, too. Ken had only been working in the Bradford office building two weeks, and he already knew Peter had had affairs with three secretaries and had been caught nailing one of the bookkeepers in a stall in the men's bathroom last year. Could she really not know?

Of course, it was possible Peter had been on the straight and narrow since meeting his fiancée. What man would want anyone else with Pamela Bradford in his life?

"Horse's ass," he muttered under his breath as Peter began untying the prostitute's halter top with his teeth. "She could do *so* much better than you."

Ken wondered why he thought so much about a woman he'd never formally met. But he did. He thought about her quite a lot, particularly when sitting in meetings in her father's office, glancing at her photo and catching glimpses of a hint of wicked humor in her wide eyes.

Pamela Bradford had sparked something in him. He'd like to call himself a gentleman and say it was his chivalrous side, rearing up in protest of the colossal mistake she was about to make. But he had to concede it was more than that. His libido definitely had something to do with it, too.

He had a serious case of the hots for his client's

daughter...and they'd never exchanged as much as a nod of hello. In the two weeks he'd been in Miami, working on a major software project for her father, he'd seen Pamela Bradford's picture on a daily basis, heard her name on her father's proud yet frustrated lips dozens of times, and seen her in the flesh once. Just once. But what an impression she'd made.

She'd just emerged from her father's office where, he'd learned later, she and Jared Bradford had argued again over Pamela's job. Jared had often moaned to Ken that his daughter, who'd been offered every advantage two doting, wealthy parents could provide, had never willingly accepted a thing from them.

Her father was afraid for her, plain and simple. She worked with inner-city kids at a teen center in Miami. The distance from her family's pricey estate in Fort Lauderdale went way beyond the mileage on I-95. It was like a different world. Pamela had chosen that world—which was completely foreign to her father.

That day, Ken had leaned against the doorjamb of his temporary office, which had been provided by the company for the duration of the three-month-long project. Arms crossed, he'd unabashedly listened to the raised voices from the next room. He'd watched as Pamela literally burst out of the heavy, oak-paneled door to her father's private sanctum, giving it a solid kick with the heel of her sneaker for good measure, before she stalked away toward the elevators.

She'd been magnificent, from the curves in her tall, lean body, to the flash of fire in her huge brown eyes. A sheen of light from the overhead fixtures cast highlights of red and gold on her chestnut-colored hair. Ken had simply stood silently, watching. She hadn't even seen him, but he'd paid close attention to her. Her chin was as proud and firm as her father's, and her shoulders were stiff under her simple green shirt. She also had a gorgeous, wide mouth made for smiling. And kissing. And...more.

It wasn't just the Pamela he saw with his own eyes that so attracted Ken. It was also the Pamela he saw through her father's eyes—through his stories, his commiserations and his fond remembrances—a woman who was stubborn, yet full of heart. That Pamela sounded like someone he'd very much like to get to know.

Unfortunately, she was about to become the wife of an oversexed moron.

"Go, go, go, go," the men around him chanted, drawing Ken's attention back to the party. Peter was chugging again, cheered on by the crowd. After the groom drained the bottle, he threw his arms up in the air like a college jock and howled.

And Pamela was marrying *him?*

Ken walked through the living area, dodging puddles of spilled beer, looking for his suit jacket. He'd taken it off when he arrived, and knew he'd left it on the back of a chair near the door. It wasn't there now. Several more guests had come in and someone had obviously done some jacket rearranging.

Frustrated, Ken looked around and saw the door to the suite open yet again. Another of the groomsmen,

who'd left earlier to find cigarettes, yelled from the hallway, "Look what I found waiting around the corner."

The man turned away, pulling at something, his already alcohol-reddened face beading with sweat. Interested in spite of himself, Ken watched as the man
pulled a cart into the room.

The cart, it appeared, had other ideas. It was pulling
back. From where he stood, Ken was able to see one
high-heeled red shoe sticking out from beneath what
appeared to be a large white-iced paper cake. The shoe
tried to stop the cart by digging into the floor. The
spiked heel, however, slid through the plush weave of
the ivory carpeting like a knife through soft butter.

Whoever the lady was, she didn't seem quite ready
for her performance. Ken could even hear her hissing at
the man to put her back where he'd found her. No one
else seemed to notice.

"The entertainment has arrived," the man said as he
finally managed to pull the large cart and cake into the
room.

The two blondes exchanged amused looks. "You're
gonna like Nona, sweetheart," one of them said to the
groom, who responded by pulling her onto his lap.

Ken, still closest to the cake, heard the person inside
say, "I need to get out of here. There's been a mistake!"

The man who'd pushed the cart in—Ken thought he
was Dan from Billing—leaned close to the *P* in the word
"Peter" written in red icing. "Don't be shy, sweetie!"

She wouldn't come out.

"Maybe she needs music," someone said doubtfully.
Considering the stereo was blasting loud enough to

shake the walls, Ken wondered what *that* guy was smoking!

Dan from Billing tried again. "Hello in there," he said. This time he poked two fingers into the side of the top tier of the paper cake, probably about level with where the dancer's face was. Ken hoped she hadn't lost an eye.

Dan nearly lost a finger. "Ouch!" he yelped as he yanked his hand free. "I think she bit me!"

Biting? Strippers? Prostitutes? Okay, Ken had seen enough. It was time to leave before they started bringing in the livestock.

But he still hadn't found his jacket. Since his car keys and phone were in the pocket, he didn't think he was going to be able to just ditch it. Walking into the kitchen area of the suite, he glanced around and began digging through a pile of coats someone had dumped on the counter.

He kept an eye on the party. Dan and another guest pulled the reluctant cart farther into the room, so it was practically right in front of the groom. Though the men tried to coax the dancer out, Peter didn't seem too concerned about his entertainer's reluctance. "We've got all night," he said with a chuckle. The blonde on his lap curled tighter against him.

"Better make it worthwhile, Pete, since it's your last night of freedom," one of the men said. Ken, who'd just about given up finding his coat, grabbed a canned soda from a cooler and rolled up his shirt sleeves. The room was getting hot and he imagined whoever the woman in the cake was, she was going to be wilted and steamy if she hid in there much longer.

"I don't think I'm going to miss my freedom much once I get my hands on my new wife. Holding her off has been killing me!"

That got Ken's attention like nothing else this evening had. It almost sounded like Peter was saying he and his bride hadn't anticipated their wedding night, which would be a shock given the groom's notorious sexual escapades.

The blonde giggled. "You mean you haven't..."

"No. Princess has to be a virgin on her wedding night or Daddy won't be happy, and that's all that counts. After waiting this long, she better make tomorrow night worthwhile."

Though Pamela wasn't here, couldn't know what was being said, Ken felt a sharp pang of embarrassment for her. This jerk was spouting off locker-room talk about the woman he was going to marry! Not only that, he was talking to a roomful of men who got their paychecks every week from that woman's father.

"Whaddya mean keeping Daddy happy?" one of the less intoxicated guys asked.

Peter's beer consumption must have been pretty high, because he answered the question, not noticing or not caring how much of an insensitive ass his answer made him appear. "She comes with the keys to the kingdom. As long as I keep her pregnant, at home and away from those dregs from the inner city she's so devoted to, I write my own ticket with dear old Dad-in-law. He and I have something of a 'gentleman's agreement.'"

Ken felt sick on Pamela's behalf. Because it sounded, from what Peter was saying, like Pamela's own father had conspired with her fiancé to get her to give up her career and be the good little socialite wife. As much as he liked Jared Bradford, Ken had to concede that as far as Pamela went, the man probably wouldn't be above such meddling.

"You can't imagine the hell I've gone through—my wife's gonna be a wild one in bed, I can tell. Practically every time I've dropped her off lately she's given me this pouty look with those lips of hers, and I've had to go cruising for some female company before I could go home!"

Ken shook his head in disgust. Of course Peter hadn't curbed his appetites in the months since his engagement. He was an oversexed *cheating* moron.

As far as Ken was concerned, once you put a ring on a woman's finger, you've promised her you'll be faithful. It was like shaking a man's hand over a business deal. You don't welch, you don't whine. You give your word to a colleague that you'll accept his offer? You stick to it. You're engaged to a woman but can't have sex till the wedding night? You start enjoying cold showers and get damned friendly with your hand. You *don't* cheat.

Shaking his head, he gave one more quick glance around the room, again looking for his coat. Then he noticed something funny. The cake was shaking. It had started to tilt a bit, and now, from here behind the cart,

Ken could see the back jerking as if the person inside was pounding on it. Slowly. Rhythmically.

"If I'd known old man Bradford was that hot for someone to take the girl off his hands, I'da tried a lot harder to get her to go out with me," someone said.

"As if you didn't already try enough—to the point that you made a complete idiot of yourself every time she walked by your cubicle," another man replied. "Not that I blame you. She's not hard on the eyes— she's got legs that'd make a man weep."

"Not to mention her sweet..."

Ken didn't hear the last word because, suddenly, the cake erupted. Two fists punched through the paper and icing on the flat top, putting holes through the *C* in "Congratulations" and the *R* in "Peter." The arms scissored, effectively slicing the paper down the middle, and a woman's head and torso burst through the opening.

"Oh, crap," someone muttered. Ken understood why as soon as he saw that thick mass of chestnut-brown hair, held in a loose clasp at the nape of her neck.

Pamela Bradford, who had obviously heard every word uttered since she'd been pushed into the room, emerged from the remains of the cake like a vengeful goddess.

2

PAMELA WASN'T THINKING, wasn't quite coherent and probably wasn't even completely sane when she burst out of the cake. She was acting on instinct, driven by rage-induced adrenaline. Thought played no part. She'd certainly never have made the conscious decision to emerge from the cake, dressed as she was, in front of a roomful of men.

When the drunken fool who'd found the cake had brought her in, Pamela had sent up every prayer she knew that her bridesmaids would come to her rescue. She'd stayed snug inside, peeking through the holes left by the man who'd tried to coax her out, wondering how darn long it could take them to find a bar in a beach-front hotel in a party town like Fort Lauderdale!

Seeing her fiancé holding a blond hooker had started her blood temperature rising. But she'd waited, giving him the benefit of the doubt, knowing it was his bachelor party. The woman had probably just planted herself on his lap.

Then he'd begun groping her.

She'd been furious, watching in sick disbelief. Her fiancé was feeling up some woman less than twelve hours before he was set to marry her. The fingers that had never once touched a single part of Pamela's body, other than her hands or a casual squeeze around her waist, had been buried in the plump folds of flesh exposed by the blond floozy's leather miniskirt. She'd begun to have major doubts about the whole wedding thing even before the stupid fathead had opened his mouth.

Once he'd done that...well, Pamela's blood had gone from simmer to raging boil in a matter of seconds. She'd been no more able to stay inside that cake than a volcano full of molten lava could keep from erupting. And erupt she did.

"Pamela," Peter exclaimed as she burst through the top with enough force to shatter the tack-wood cake frame into tiny pieces. Peter pushed the blonde off his lap so fast she landed in a heap at his feet.

"Shut up, Peter. Just shut up," Pamela ordered as she pushed her way through the paper and sticky icing, feeling it matting in her hair and smearing onto her thighs. Her foot got stuck under the cart shelf where she'd been sitting. Pamela had to tug it free, silently cursing the shoes, her fiancé, her father and her life.

Peter reached out a hand. "Pamela, let me explain."

"Touch me and I'll rip your arm off," she snarled, feeling it was entirely possible she could do just that.

"Darling..."

"I'm not your darling!" Pamela finally got her foot free and stepped over the legs of the blonde, who watched with wide eyes from her position on the floor. "I was never your darling. And I'm not my father's princess. So you can go tell the king the wedding's off! I guess that makes you the jester, huh, Peter?"

She glared at every man in the room, noting that most of them dropped their eyes, ashamed to meet her stare. She didn't suppose a single one of them had been too ashamed to look away when she'd first gotten out of the cake. No, she imagined they'd gotten quite an eyeful. Her face flushed scarlet and she tugged the filmy pink shirt tightly around her body, crossing her arms in front of her chest.

Slowly, the men began turning away. Some reached for coats, some left the living area altogether, going toward another room in the suite. She ignored them and began walking toward the door.

"Please, Pamela, don't be rash. You misunderstood."

"I heard you perfectly well, Peter," she replied as she reached the foyer. "My father hired you, coached you on how to get me interested and promised you a big payoff for pretending you were madly in love." Her voice broke, and she forced herself to straighten her shoulders. "What's not to understand?"

He took a step toward her. "It wasn't like that."

Pamela pointed her index finger at him. "Ah-ah. I meant it. Don't you come near me. Maybe it won't be your *arm* I rip off."

Peter visibly gulped. Hearing one of the men chuckle, Pamela swung her gaze toward them. Most were still huddled in the back corner, near the interior hallway. There was also apparently some kind of kitchen area that she couldn't see, and she figured more of the weasels were huddled in there, listening to every word, peeking around corners or through archways like the nasty little vermin they were.

She'd never forget their laughter, the way they cheered Peter on, seemingly proud of him for his plan. She'd never forget their faces, knowing they probably derived some sort of satisfaction in her humiliation, since so many of them had made a play for her at one time or another. Yes, she imagined they were enjoying seeing her brought down to size.

Tears filled her eyes. She blinked them back, determined not to let a single one fall free of her lashes—at least not until after she got out of this room, away from their knowing faces, far from the echo of Peter's sickeningly self-satisfied voice.

From where she lay on the floor, the blonde cleared her throat. Forcing herself into a surreal sense of calm despite the raging intensity building inside her, Pamela met the woman's eye. "You have something to contribute to this conversation?"

"Them are Nona's favorite shoes you got on," the woman said matter-of-factly as she stared at Pamela's legs.

Not pausing, Pamela bent down and slipped one then the other of the glittery red spike-heeled pumps off her feet. She gently tossed one into the center of the room. The heel caught in the remnants of the cake and hung there, dangling inches above the floor. The other shoe flew out of her hand with a bit more speed and precision. It caught Peter right in the middle of his gut. He bent forward, gasping for air. Pamela was unable to stop a snort of satisfaction as she reached for the door handle.

Pamela opened the door, but before she stepped out

of the suite, she paused and looked back at her former fiancé. Peter looked unsteady. He still breathed deeply, swaying and blinking hard, as if unable to believe everything he'd worked so hard for was collapsing around him in a matter of ninety seconds. His shoulders slumped, and he raised a hand to cover his eyes. The hooker watched from below. The cowardly men still huddled in their corners.

"Oh, Peter?" Pamela called sweetly.

He immediately lowered his hand and looked toward her, a faint light of hopefulness in his beady little eyes that had once seemed so truthful and gentle.

Once she was sure she had his full attention, Pamela gave him a wicked smile. Uncrossing her arms, she tugged the filmy shirt open, flashing him. His jaw fell open.

"You're an idiot," she said as she ran one flat palm across the curve of her hip, concealed only by the thin red strap of her thong panties.

"And I'm definitely *not* a virgin."

THOSE IN THE SUITE remained silent after Pamela slammed out, as if the reverberations of the door had frozen them where they stood. In the kitchen, Ken was as shocked by her sudden appearance—and disappearance—as everyone else. Her parting shot hung in the air, though Ken knew he, Peter and the prostitute were the only ones who could have seen her last defiant gesture.

It took a half minute before Ken could breathe again. He'd only caught a glimpse of Pamela through the leaves of an artificial plant hanging in an arched opening between the kitchen and living room. But he'd never forget the sight of her. Never.

She was, quite simply, glorious. The tawdry costume that should have appeared cheap had been heart-poundingly enticing instead. There was too much class in the woman, from her proud shoulders to the line of her jaw and the arch of her brow, for her ever to appear less than a lady.

He didn't think he'd ever seen a more beautifully shaped woman—not in magazines, not in the flesh. The full curve of her hips begged for a man's hands, while the sweet indentation of her belly cried out to be kissed. And the long line of her thighs invited hours of delightful exploration.

But it was the pain in her eyes that spoke to Ken's soul.

"Screw the coat," he muttered as he stepped out of the kitchen to go after her. No way was he going to just stand there while she ran through the hotel, dressed like that, devastated and alone. He might not know her. He did, however, know hurt when he saw it, and the woman needed someone to help her deal with what had happened.

As he stepped by, the blond hooker slowly rose from the floor. "She a workin' girl? She sure got the body for it."

Peter looked stunned. "How could this have happened?"

Ken gave him a frown of disdain. His fingers curled into a fist; he itched to slug the man in the jaw, even if

Pamela wasn't here anymore to need protecting. Though sorely tempted, he refrained, wanting nothing more than to get out of the suite.

When he glanced at the chair where Peter and his ladyfriend had been sitting, he spotted his jacket and grabbed it.

"You sure she don't dance? Gawd, she could be making some big bucks," the blonde said.

Peter shook his head. "Why didn't I *do* her when I had the chance?"

This time Ken didn't listen to any inner voice of reason. He answered Peter's question with his fist.

AFTER PAMELA slammed out of the suite, she had to stop for a moment, in the empty, silent hotel hall. She leaned her forehead against the wall as the tears built in her eyes, the sobs choked her chest, and the hot rage completely gave way to pain and humiliation.

She gave herself no more than a few seconds to wallow. Then she dashed down the empty corridor. Ignoring the elevator, she burst through the door to the stairs instead. There, safe for the moment from prying eyes, she hugged her arms tightly around her body and gave in to tears.

"You rotten bastard," she muttered. Only she didn't know who she was talking to at that moment. Peter? Or her father? Which one had hurt her more? Which one had thrust the knife into her heart, and which had turned it?

She didn't have to think about it for long. Her father was the one who really loved her. So he was the one who'd really betrayed her. And she was never going to forgive him for it.

Nor would she ever forgive herself. Stupid! She'd been such a fool to let Peter get away with his scheme. God, she'd almost *married* the man!

Amazingly, there was no emotional pain at the loss of her fiancé yet. There was pain, oh, yes, but it was pain at being used, at being made a fool of. Mostly at being betrayed by her father. There was also anger, embarrassment and shock.

But did her heart hurt? Was she emotionally devastated? Not yet. At least not as much as she'd expect to be upon learning the man she was pretty doggone sure she loved had been using her.

Maybe that would come later. Or maybe she wasn't so doggone sure after all, and it wouldn't. Whatever the case, the one thing she *did* feel was humiliation.

After several minutes, Pamela descended the stairwell, wondering where Sue, Wanda and LaVyrle were. She didn't want to see them; she didn't want to see anyone who might demand an explanation. Pamela just wanted to find something to pull on over the ridiculous stripper's outfit and go home. Since she'd left her purse, money, clothes and car keys in the locked trunk of LaVyrle's car, she didn't see much chance of that happening anytime soon.

The stairwell ended near a back elevator, not far from the lobby. Nearby, Pamela heard the sounds of laughter and tinkling glasses from the hotel bar, and she wondered if her bridesmaids—ex-bridesmaids—were there. Doubtful. They'd probably already gone upstairs, discovered the cake cart was missing, and were wondering where she was.

Pamela took a few seconds to indulge a fantasy of how LaVyrle would react if she went into the suite and heard what had happened. "Wonder if Peter's health insurance is paid up," she whispered with an evil grin. Thinking of his pride in his big, white, flashy smile, she hoped LaVyrle went for the mouth.

The lobby was nearly deserted, but she had to assume someone was working behind the check-in counter. That person would be unlikely to miss a half-naked woman running toward the exit. Pamela avoided the lobby.

She also steered clear of the bar. As much as she would have loved a good stiff drink, she couldn't exactly see going in and ordering one. Nor could she have paid for it. "Bet someone would buy me one," she muttered sourly.

Instead, she made her way out the back door of the hotel, which obviously led to the pool area and the beach. Sending up a silent prayer that some careless tourist had forgotten an old T-shirt or cover-up, she prowled around in the darkness.

"Bingo!" she chortled when she found a colorful beach towel lying forgotten near the kiddie pool. It was better than nothing, and she wrapped it around herself, covering the obscenely thin shirt and spangled undergarments.

With no one around, no money and no means of transportation, Pamela knew she was going to have to call for help. But who to call? Her best friends were somewhere inside the hotel. Her ex-fiancé was probably consoling himself in the arms of the hooker.

That thought sent another chill through her body, and Pamela realized she wasn't ready to see anyone she knew yet. She needed to be alone, to think, to absorb what had happened and what she was going to do about it.

"Well, the wedding's off, first of all," she muttered aloud.

Stepping away from the pool, she glanced at the wooden steps that led down to the beach. The gently lapping waves and the glimmer of moonlight shining on the surface of the water offered peace and seclusion, a way to soothe her turbulent emotions.

Without even hesitating, she walked down the steps onto the beach. The sand, cooled by the night air, felt sharp against her bare feet. Closing her eyes, she inhaled deeply, trying to remember the relaxation techniques Sue had taught her when her friend had been going through her "female empowerment" stage. That had been between Sue's stages of "I'm going to astronaut training school" and "I'm going to get artificially inseminated and raise a baby by myself".

"Focus on the sensations of each moment," Pamela reminded herself. "Think about nothing but the salty taste of the air on your lips, the froth of the waves lapping your feet, the churning surf filling your ears."

She closed her eyes, trying to focus. It worked for about six seconds. Then she snorted in disgust because all she could think about was her lying, cheating bastard of an ex-fiancé.

"You rotten louse!" she shouted to the sky, knowing no one was nearby to hear her. Shouting made her feel better. Punching something would have helped, too.

Pamela didn't realize she wasn't alone on the beach until someone spoke.

"Have we met?"

Shocked, she opened her eyes and jerked her attention over her shoulder. A man stood behind her, a few feet away on the beach. He watched her, nearly hidden by the shadow of the nearby dune crossover.

"No," Pamela said, casting a quick look around to see if she could spot anyone else. This wasn't exactly a safe situation. She stood, nearly undressed, on a dark beach, late at night, and a strange man was behind her. *Uh-oh.*

"How can you know I'm a louse then?" he asked.

She frowned. "I wasn't talking to you. I was having a private moment."

"Looked more like a private meltdown," he said.

As he stepped closer, out of the shadows and into the light cast by the streetlamp above them in the parking lot, Pamela got her first good look at him. She sucked in a breath, more concerned than she'd been before.

He wore the south Florida businessman's summer uniform. A white dress shirt, with sleeves rolled up, revealed thick, tanned forearms. He wore no tie, and his shirt collar was undone, displaying a neck corded with muscle and the hint of dark hair at the hollow of his throat. Though he also wore light-colored trousers, and carried a matching suit jacket slung over one shoulder, Pamela knew this was no normal happy-hour executive out for a late-night stroll. The blasé businessman clothes lied.

He was all dark intensity. From the thick hair—likely black though she couldn't be sure in this light—that curled past his collar, to the piercing darkness of his eyes, he defied the image of polished executive that her ex-fiancé had cultivated. The strong line of his determined jaw warned of a man who wouldn't be easily coerced. The thickness of his arms and the breadth of his chest told of his strength.

He looked like a cop, or a soldier.

But as those amazingly well-defined lips curled upward into a teasing smile, she realized he did *not* look like an ax-murdering rapist. She managed to smile a little in response.

"Okay, I'm having a private meltdown. The key word being private."

"I take it you want me to take a hike?"

"If you please," she said, tugging the beach towel tighter around her body and turning her attention toward the surf.

She sensed his hesitation and glanced at him. He pointed toward her head. "Did you know you've got a clump of white stuff in your hair?"

Pamela reached a hand up and dug a fistful of icing off the top of her head and threw it into the surf.

"Rough night?"

"Beyond belief," she said with a snort.

"Anything I can do?"

"Not unless you're a hit man."

The man didn't seem shocked. "Sorry," he said with

a rueful smile. "Forgot my assassin gear. I guess you're out of luck."

"Now there's an understatement! Tonight has been just about the worst night I've ever experienced. All I want is my bed and a good stiff one."

The man laughed out loud, obviously hearing a sexy submeaning in her innocent comment.

"I mean a good stiff drink!"

"Yeah, I knew that," he said, trying hard to keep a straight face. The grin on his lips begged for a response, and Pamela's own smile widened.

"I'm not trying to flirt with you," she said, trying to sound stern, but laughing instead.

"Good thing, because you'd be doing a pretty pathetic job," he said. "I mean, first the louse thing, then you basically told me to get lost."

"Which you didn't do."

"Touché. Do you still want me to go?"

For some reason, though she'd come down to the beach to be alone, she found herself wanting him to stay. There was something so appealing about his crooked grin, the self-deprecating laugh and the warmth of his stare.

A few minutes with a stranger on a dark secluded beach. She could think of worse ways to spend what should have been the night before her wedding.

"You'd probably be better off leaving," she muttered ruefully. "I'm not great company right now. As a matter of fact, I'm pretty miserable."

"Not thinking of pulling a *Jaws* scene, are you?" he

asked, looking at her bare feet, then at the surf lapping closer toward them on the sand.

"No. I'm not going for a late-night swim. I'm, uh...just thinking. It's been a pretty bad night and, to top it all off, I now find myself stranded, without my purse, real clothes or a buck to buy a beer I can cry into."

Surprisingly, the man didn't ask about the clothes comment. Instead, he reached into the pocket of his sports coat and drew out a few minibottles of whiskey. "Would this help?"

Though she wasn't ordinarily a drinker, Pamela grabbed for a bottle, unsealed it and took a hefty sip.

"I hate this stuff," she said between choking coughs after she swallowed. The rush of warmth descended from her throat to her belly, and Pamela took it in, needing it to calm her nerves. Another sip brought the same reaction. This time, as she bent over in a small coughing fit, the towel came untucked and fell open. She snatched it back up, covering herself, looking at the man to see if he'd noticed.

He didn't comment on her clothes—or lack thereof. Instead, he took his suit jacket off his shoulder and held it out to her. "Here. At least it won't fall off."

Pamela stared at his hand, and the jacket, wondering why his simple, chivalrous offer brought tears to her eyes. She looked up at him, trying to find an indication of his thoughts in his expression. She saw only kindness. Concern. A gentle look of tenderness in eyes that she sensed could sometimes be as cold as a gray winter's sky. But tonight, under the light of the glowing moon and what seemed to be a million stars reflecting off the water, they were infused with warmth.

"Thank you," she whispered, taking the jacket from his hand. He turned slightly, so that he faced the ocean. When she saw him avert his gaze, she knew he was offering her privacy. She took it, dropping the towel and slipping the jacket on over her shoulders. "You really are a gentleman. Unlike every other man I've run across this evening."

From where he stood, silently watching the surf as she donned his coat, Ken cringed. She'd sounded very bitter when she talked about the other men she'd spent the evening with. He had to imagine she was never going to forgive Peter's friends, the men who had witnessed what had happened in the suite.

How the hell could he tell her he was *one* of them?

"I don't know about that," he murmured finally. "But at least I know I'm not a louse."

Which she should feel pretty damn lucky about. Standing out here at almost midnight, dressed as she was, the lady could have found herself in some very serious trouble if the wrong kind of man had happened by.

"No, the louse...or is it lice?" she said with a bitter laugh, "would be my ex-fiancé and his friends. Plus my father."

"So it's not all males you're hating at this moment?"

"No. Just a handful," she admitted as she took another drink from the small bottle, draining it.

He took the empty bottle from her and watched as she popped open the second one. "Easy there."

"I'm entitled. You can't imagine the night I've had."

Actually, he could. But he wasn't about to tell her that. Pamela's embarrassment was already easy enough to see. If he told her he'd witnessed her entire humiliation, she'd stalk away from him. Now, after she'd had a drink, she would probably be even more vulnerable than she'd been before! He was thankful he'd been the one to find her after he'd left the party, leaving Peter laid out on the carpet behind him.

Ken flexed his hand, thankful he hadn't broken any fingers. Whatever bruises or stiffness he had tomorrow would be well worth the satisfaction he'd gotten knocking Peter on his arrogant ass. He hadn't stuck around to see how long it took the other man to get up. He'd been totally focused on finding Pamela.

She hadn't been hard to locate. How many places were there in a beachfront hotel for a half-naked female to hide? Certainly not the bar or the restaurant. He'd doubted she'd booked a room. There had been no place she could have possibly concealed any cash, ID or keys in that getup she'd been wearing, so he didn't imagine she'd hopped into a cab or her car.

Putting himself in her shoes, er, her bare feet, he'd figured the beach was where he'd have gone. He hadn't been surprised that was where he'd found her. "So, want to talk about it?" He looked back at her, raising a quizzical eyebrow.

She shrugged. "My name's Pamela Bradford. Tomorrow was supposed to be my wedding day."

"And what, you and the groom argued over the wedding cake and started throwing icing around?" he said, trying to make her laugh, trying to avoid letting her know that he knew all about the cake incident.

"That's not so far from the truth," she muttered glumly.

Ken didn't know Pamela very well—heck, he didn't know her at all. But he had three younger sisters. Growing up, all three of them had considered him the representative for every male on the planet, heaping all the praises—but, more often, all the sins—of his sex right on top of his head.

One thing he'd learned—aside from never going near his sister Diana's chocolate stash around the time of the full moon—was that in moments of emotional crisis, females needed to get things off their chest or they'd explode. Not wanting his boss's daughter blown to a million bits on a Fort Lauderdale beach, he urged her on. "So tell me all about your wedding plans."

She snorted. "They're off!"

"The wedding's been called off?"

"Well, unofficially, yes. I guess I'll leave it to Peter to explain to all our guests why the bride couldn't make it."

Ken glanced at his watch. "He's going to have to come up with a reason pretty quick...or will he tell them the truth?"

"That he's a womanizing jerk who basically accepted a bribe from my father to get me to marry him?"

Ken winced at the anger in her voice. "Guess not."

Suddenly, without warning, Pamela was spilling out the whole story. Her childhood. Her relationship with her parents. Her dedication to her job, which had her interacting on a daily basis with teenagers the city of Miami seemed disinclined to help. She even told him about her disillusionment with her fiancé.

Ken listened, finally understanding why Pamela would ever have gotten involved with a guy like Peter Weiss. The man had played her like an instrument, using her father's advice on her likes and dislikes to appeal to her. How could any woman resist a man who agreed with every word she said, who was completely supportive and anticipated her every need?

"Didn't that get boring? A guy who never said no to you?"

"It wasn't like that," she retorted. "There was security in knowing we were so much alike."

"Sounds like a yawnfest." Ken shrugged. "Stepford Groom."

"So what would you know about it?" she retorted, her fist on her hip. "Are you a relationship expert or something?"

"Nope. My relationships have basically blown lately."

She raised an eyebrow.

"But I do know I would never be able to stand being with a woman who agreed with every word I said!"

"As if that'd ever happen," she muttered, seeming to forget her own problems for the moment.

"Are you saying I'm difficult to get along with? And here I thought I'd been the soul of cordiality."

She suddenly looked contrite. "You have. I'm so sorry. You've been wonderful, and I don't even know your name. I didn't mean to be critical. It's just that the men in my life have been less than sterling lately."

Ken knew without her saying it that she spoke more about her father than she did about Peter Weiss. Ken was not surprised to realize she seemed even more devastated by her father's involvement than she did by Peter's actions.

"My name's Ken."

A wicked grin crossed her face. "My Barbie dolls always preferred G.I. Joe."

"My G.I. Joe always preferred Wonder Woman," he retorted without missing a beat.

She laughed out loud for the first time since they'd met on the beach and Ken felt the sand shift under his feet. Odd. But it happened. The ground moved a bit, his breath grew heavy in his lungs, and he couldn't tear his stare away from her wide, smiling mouth. *This* was the Pamela he'd longed to meet.

"I once traded my scooter for a G.I. Joe doll. My father caught me playing 'G.I. Joe beats the crap out of Ken for trying to force Barbie to be a model rather than an astronaut.'"

Ken grinned. "And how did your father react?"

"He flicked my Ken doll's head so hard it flew off," she said with a sad smile that segued into a look of pain. "He used to tell me there was nothing a girl couldn't do."

Ken moved closer, tempted to take her arm, to stroke a stray wisp of fine, dark hair, dancing in the night ocean breeze, off her smooth brow. Instead, he said softly, "But now he's let you down?"

She tightened her arms around the front of his jacket, hugging it against her body. "He's been saying one thing but doing another. Sure, there was nothing I couldn't do—as long as it was something of which he approved."

"And you're sure he helped your fiancé a little bit?"

She snorted a laugh and tossed her head. "A little bit? Good grief, an Olympic coach probably wouldn't have done as good a job preparing Peter for the Pamela games!"

Her brief spurt of humor fled. Her face was again dark and troubled, and Ken regretted the change. She was thinking about her father, and Ken wondered how she'd ever be able to deal with what she viewed as his betrayal.

Jared Bradford loved her. Ken knew that perfectly well. But he couldn't reassure her of that. He couldn't ask her to admit that while her father's actions might have been reprehensible, they weren't malicious. Admitting he knew her father would mean telling her why he was at the hotel.

"Getting chilly out here. Do you mind?" He pointed toward the whiskey bottles in the pocket of his own jacket, which she still wore. He didn't really want a drink. But it seemed wise to reduce the supply so Pamela wouldn't drown her sorrows by drinking every single one of them.

Since the jacket pocket was just about even with one of her curvy hips, he did *not* reach out to help himself. *Touch her and you're a goner!*

"I think I've had enough," she finally said, studying the empty container in her hand.

Considering she'd downed two by herself, he thought she was right.

"But help yourself," she continued, pulling one of the remaining miniatures out of the pocket and handing it to him.

Ken took it from her fingers, noting the coolness of her smooth, pale skin against the slick glass. He took a quick step back, then busied himself opening the bottle.

"So, Peter pretended to be the perfect guy...but why on earth did you feel the need to show up at his bachelor party and jump out of his cake?" Ken asked, still not completely clear on what had led up to this evening's performance.

She sighed. "I don't know. The way it turned out, it would have almost been easier to accept if Peter was gay."

Ken almost choked on a sip of the whiskey. "You thought your fiancé was *gay?*"

"No," she insisted. "I didn't think so! My friends wondered if he might be, though, when I told them that I'd never...that he'd never...uh..."

"You weren't lovers," he stated, still feeling like a slimeball for not admitting that he'd witnessed the entire awful scene in the hotel.

"No," she replied, a note of defiance in her voice. "He seemed to think that I was destined to be pure as the driven snow on my wedding night, and my father insisted I remain that way. Thank God he did— at least I never slept with the creep!"

Ken nearly echoed the sentiment.

One thing Pamela hadn't mentioned during all her explanations was her one final, defiant gesture as she'd left the party. Not that he was surprised. He didn't know many women who'd have had the nerve to do what she'd done—and then talk about it!

"So," he asked as he put the cap back on the miniature bottle, "you going to give your father a chance to explain?"

"Nope," she replied succinctly.

"Are you going to at least tell him there's not going to be any wedding tomorrow?"

She scowled, looking as though she wanted to do just that. Then her shoulders drooped. "Do you have a cell phone?"

"Right-hand pocket."

He watched her pull his phone from his jacket and dial some numbers. She took a few deep breaths, looking up at the stars overhead while she waited for an answer. Ken watched, knowing the pain this phone call would reveal—and the pain it would inflict. Though he hated what Jared had done to his daughter, Ken knew how much the man loved her. This was gonna be bad.

"Hello, Daddy? No, no, I'm fine. Yes, I know what time it is." She looked at her wrist, but she wore no watch. Ken held his arm toward her and showed her his.

"No, please listen," she continued. "I want to tell you I hope you and your five hundred friends have a wonderful time eating the surf and turf tomorrow afternoon at the club. Hope it'll be worth it. Unfortunately, I won't

be there so I'll have to count on everyone else to tell me
how the reception goes. Be sure to have someone save
me a piece of *cake*."

She laughed, a desperate sound that held no joy. "Oh,
Peter called, did he? So you understand, of course, why
there will be no wedding."

She shook her head. "No. Dad, I don't want to hear it.
I don't want to hear a single word you have to say." Her
voice caught with unshed tears. "You betrayed me—
Peter used me, but *you* betrayed me."

She cut the connection, turned off the phone, and
promptly burst into tears.

3

MOST MEN didn't know how to react when a woman burst into tears right in front of them. Ken, however, had a little experience. Resorting to basics, he grabbed her by the shoulders and pulled her into his arms.

She cried until his shirt became warm and damp with her tears, but she made no move to step away. He ran a consoling palm down her back, cupped her head with his hand and tried to ignore the rush of physical pleasure he got out of holding her in his arms.

She fit very well against him. Since she was nearly as tall as he, her cheek brushed against his neck as she cried. His pants and dress shirt provided a layer of fabric between them, but he felt her curves against his body. The delicate perfume she wore competed with the lingering sweet scent of icing. With her head tucked into his shoulder, Ken found his lips next to her temple and was unable to resist placing a soft, consoling kiss there. His fingers tangled in her hair as he held her and he finally started to feel her relax.

Comfort gradually segued into something else. She drew in a few deep breaths. He felt the pulse in her temple beat faster as she acknowledged the intimacy of their embrace. Anyone watching from the crossover above would have thought them passionate lovers.

"I'm sorry," she muttered against his shoulder. "I can't believe I'm sobbing in the arms of a complete stranger."

"Well, in the absence of a beer to cry into..."

She pulled away from him and took a step back, wiping her cheeks with the backs of her hands. Her makeup was smeared under her eyes and her face was puffy. "I'm usually not a cryer."

"It's okay, really. I'm glad I was here."

"You won't be when you see the black circles my mascara made on your shirt," she said glumly. "If you give it to me, I'll be happy to have it cleaned."

She looked miserable. Ken wanted to see that smile again, wanted to move past the sudden moment of intense awareness that had flashed between them while she remained in his arms. "You're just determined to get all my clothes off me, aren't you?"

She raised an eyebrow, obviously hearing the teasing in his flirtatious remark. Her reply, however, wasn't quite so teasing.

"Is it working?"

That surprised him. Ken wondered if she heard the blatant suggestiveness in her own voice. He doubted it. Even if she did, he certainly wouldn't take it seriously. The woman was right smack-dab in rebound territory—and Ken had already had his one experience with a woman fresh from a breakup with someone else. It had ended with a *Dear Ken* letter. He'd vowed never to put himself in that position again. She needed a friend? Okay. She needed a sounding board? He could be that, too.

She needed a warm and willing pair of arms to make her forget her miserable love life? *Been there, done that. Pick another guy, lady.*

He gave her a noncommittal smile. "I think I can manage to wash the shirt."

She shrugged. "That's about how my love life's been lately. Can't get a man to even want to take off his shirt for me."

Ken almost barked out a laugh. Then he realized that while her tone was light, her expression was very serious. "You can't honestly still be thinking your fiancé didn't want you. Not now that you know why he was staying away from you."

She turned slightly, facing the water and looking down at her hands. "I obviously didn't offer much temptation." Apparently seeing his confusion, she hurried on, "Not that I'm not very glad we never went any further! It's just..."

"Yes?"

"Well, let's say my track record with men isn't so great. Not many guys are too hot for a five foot ten former basketball jock who now fights and claws through bureaucratic b.s., dealers, gangs and absentee parents every day in her job."

"Only men with brains to go with their...libido," he said.

She crossed her arms in front of her chest. "I've learned to accept the fact that I'll never be mistaken for a femme fatale."

Remembering what she looked like under that jacket, Ken had to bite his tongue to hold back a retort. As he watched, Pamela reached into the pocket of his jacket and drew out the last small bottle of alcohol. "You're sure you want that?"

She opened the bottle and lifted it to her lips. "Hey, it's my wedding day. Doesn't the almost-bride deserve a toast?" Without pause, she drained the small bottle. This time she didn't collapse into a coughing fit, though she gave one shudder and blinked her watery eyes.

"So, I guess your father's going to be out a small fortune, hm?"

She nodded. "Guess so. It's not like he can't afford it. I didn't want the country club wedding, anyway."

"What did you want, Pamela?" Ken asked, studying her profile as she watched the surf.

"Just an awesome honeymoon."

He laughed.

"You think I'm kidding? After dealing with Peter's, uh...lack of interest, I wanted to go somewhere alone and make sure we were really compatible." Pamela took a step back, wobbled a little on her feet, then bit her lip. "Do you mind if I sit down?"

"Go right ahead." He grinned, wondering how uncomfortable the sand was going to feel against the huge amount of bare skin exposed by her underclothes. Just thinking of that sent a burst of heat rushing through him. *Don't even go there!*

"So, where were you going on this honeymoon?" he asked as he sat next to her in the sand.

Pamela glanced over at him, wondering why he didn't seem to care that his trousers were probably going to be ruined by sitting on the beach. Then she remembered she was wearing his jacket. While it didn't entirely protect her fanny from the damp ground, it would more than likely be in pretty bad shape by the time she got up.

Remorseful, Pamela leaned over, holding his jacket down over her backside with the flat of her palm, and grabbed the beach towel. She spread it out and moved over to sit on it.

"Might not be too late for this suit," she offered with a grin. She patted the other half of the towel, inviting him to join her. When he did, she realized exactly how small the kiddie beach towel was. While it had wrapped once around her torso, it certainly didn't provide enough width to keep their bodies from touching, shoulder to hip, bringing every one of her senses roaring to life.

"Uh, now, what did you say?" she asked, focusing on wiggling her toes into the sand to avoid staring at the well-defined shoulder just inches from her cheek.

"I was asking about your honeymoon. Where were you going?"

"Lake Tahoe. To a gorgeous couples-only honeymoon resort called The Little Love Nest."

She heard him chuckle, then he said, "Sounds pricey. Guess Daddy's going to be out some cash on that deal, too."

His words reminded Pamela of the truth. No, her father wasn't going to be the one losing out on the small fortune her honeymoon trip had cost.

She leaned back, dropping her elbows to the sand and reclining on them, frowning in disgust. "Nope, that was all mine! Peter didn't even know about it. I paid for everything and had planned to surprise him tomorrow when we got there."

"No trip insurance?"

She snorted and cast an incredulous look at him. "Gee, do they offer insurance against jerk-off fiancés who cheat and lie?"

"Guess not."

She didn't even want to think of the amount of money she'd spent on the trip. Actually, she couldn't really think about it, because her head was a teensy bit spinny. From the alcohol. From the stress. From the nearness of this stranger whose cologne made her want to bury her face in his neck, and whose warmth made her long to crawl back into his arms.

She shook her head once, hard, trying to clear her brain. "I think maybe I shouldn't have had that last drink," she whispered as she tried to focus on sticking her toes into the damp sand. "I also think I'm going to wake up tomorrow and wonder if this whole thing was a nightmare."

"I think you'll be glad you found out tonight that your fiancé is a cheat and a liar," Ken replied, "rather than after tomorrow."

She sneaked another glance at him, liking the strength of his jaw, the quirk of his brow as he cast a knowing grin at her—not to mention the muscular neck, the broad shoulders, the long legs stretched out next to hers against the damp sand.

Pamela suddenly realized there was more than alcohol making her feel sort of funny, like she had butterflies in her stomach. She was responding to him physically. More than that, though, she found she liked him, this stranger who'd found her on the beach and somehow made her laugh on what was turning out to be the worst night of her life.

She liked his eyes, and she liked his laugh. She liked those big strong hands that had held her with such gentleness when she'd cried. *Yeah right. As if that's all she liked.*

She'd also very much liked the look of his lips and wondered if he used them for kissing as well as he used them for grinning.

The fact that they were so close together fueled her feelings. The elemental churning of the waves, and the moisture in the air brought forth a response deep within her. She suddenly found her mind filled with the most vivid picture of her and this man lying in the surf in a passionate embrace.

Now she knew she was tipsy. She was having sexual fantasies about a complete stranger! She tried to force them out of her mind, but they stayed, making her pulse beat faster, her breath come harder, and making her legs shake, though she told herself that was only because of the strong ocean breeze blowing across her. Looking at him out of the corner of her eye, she again noticed the strength of his face, the long lashes hooding his expressive eyes, and his hard body, hidden under the dress shirt and slacks.

She wanted him. "How crazy is that?" she muttered out loud, ignoring his questioning glance.

It was true. She wanted this gray-eyed man, wanted

his hands on her breasts and his mouth on her throat. Wanted him on top of her. Beneath her.

Inside her.

"Oh, goodness, I definitely had too much to drink," she whispered.

Knowing she had no business even thinking such things did not halt the thoughts. They did, however, remind her of that last scene with Peter up in the suite. She wondered where on earth she'd found the courage to do what she'd done, to say what she'd said. Because she was a big, fat liar. She'd taunted Peter that she wasn't a virgin. Whoops! Not exactly true.

As ridiculous as it seemed in this day and age, Pamela, at twenty-six, *was* a virgin.

Some people might wonder how she could have remained basically untouched all her life, but Pamela knew her upbringing and her job were the reasons. Growing up, she'd listened when her parents had talked about their respect and love for one another. Subconsciously, she'd wanted that for herself.

Considering that she was taller than nearly every guy she went to high school with, and could generally humiliate them on the basketball court, they weren't usually lining up to ask her out. The fact that her father used to like to greet the few who did dressed in old Army fatigues—sometimes while cleaning his antique gun collection—had helped too. The few guys she'd dated had been too scared to make a serious move on her. Any father was intimidating. One with lots of money probably more so. But one with money, guns and a military background? Pamela would've had a better shot at winning the lottery than graduating high school *sullied*.

College had been about study and basketball, and not necessarily in that order. Not much time for guys. Then, once she'd started working in the inner city, her job had reinforced the lessons her parents had instilled. She interacted with troubled families on a daily basis. So many of their problems involved teen pregnancies, heartbreak, divorce. She'd seen what casual sex did to young girls, and her heart ached for them as they struggled to find their way through school, career and home life while trying to raise their babies.

Pamela's mind had simply erected an invisible chastity belt around her underwear. No, she hadn't set out to remain a virgin until marriage. Nor, however, had she ever intended to let sex trap her into a life she wasn't ready for and didn't want.

That was why Peter's disinterest had so devastated her. For the first time in her life, she'd let a man know she was his for the taking—and he hadn't taken!

Okay, so Peter's kisses hadn't overwhelmed her. They'd been pretty darned interesting though. Interesting enough to get her thinking about what would come *after* the kisses.

She was ready to move on, forge ahead, experience everything a woman possibly could in terms of sensual pleasures. That was why she'd jumped on the chance to go to The Little Love Nest resort at Lake Tahoe. Not so much to encourage Peter as to give her the chance to finally revel in the sexuality she'd kept bottled up for the past twenty-six years of her life!

There was so much she hadn't done. So much she'd assumed she'd learn with her husband. Her body was crying out to experience and do all kinds of things she'd only ever fantasized about. Pamela wanted to feel feminine, sultry and seductive for the first time in her life. She was ready to give in to heady desire and lust and love and passion. She wanted to do everything lovers did. Do everything she'd dreamed about and everything she could imagine.

Only now she was short one bridegroom.

"So, what do you want to do?"

The mouthful of air Pamela had just inhaled turned into a lump of sand in her throat, and she choked on it. *Had he read her mind?* She sat up, coughing and hacking into her fist, noticing Ken's worried expression as he patted her back.

"Are you all right?"

"Yeah, I'm fine," she muttered. "Just deep in..." *lust* "...thought."

"You trying to think of a way to get your money back on your honeymoon trip?"

She shook her head, scrunching up her brow. "Not exactly. More like trying to think of a reason not to go ahead and go by myself!"

She hadn't really considered it until she'd said the words, but now couldn't imagine why she shouldn't do it. Why should she lose out on her single vacation of the year? It was paid for, wasn't it? Her time off was scheduled. What was she going to do, sit around and wallow for the next week?

He laughed for a moment, and then obviously realized she was serious. "I thought it was a honeymoon resort. Wouldn't that be kind've a downer?"

Rising to her feet, a bit unsteadily, she shrugged. "It's a spa. Relaxing. Rejuvenating. I'm sure there are lots of people I could meet."

The more she talked, the more she liked the idea. Seven days at Lake Tahoe, far from anyone who knew her, far from her job and her family and the self-imposed restrictions. Most particularly, far from her father, who couldn't scare off or try to buy a man for her.

Maybe she would meet someone amazing. Someone who had no conflicted loyalties, no knowledge of who her father even was!

She had seven days to test these physical desires that she'd buried for so long—desires that she thought would choke her if she didn't find a way to relieve them. "Lots of interesting men...people," she repeated under her breath.

"Lots of *married* men," Ken retorted as he stood up next to her and began brushing the sand off himself.

"I wouldn't be tied down to the resort," she said stubbornly. "I'll bet there are lot of places to go and people to meet."

People? Men! Men who might actually want her, not what her father offered them. What the heck, why *shouldn't* she?

Of course, there was the minor problem that the resort was vehement about being for couples only. They might frown on a swinging single bride. Maybe she could say her fiancé had been delayed and would join her later. A smile of pure evil crossed her lips. Maybe she could tell them he'd fallen out of an airplane over the Great Salt Lake.

Her smile widened and she closed her eyes. She'd meet someone there and indulge in a decadent honeymoon with a completely delicious stranger. She'd bring the outfit she was wearing, confident that he'd be unable to breathe when he watched her undress for him. Her confidence would grow under the approval in his gaze as his gray eyes darkened with desire. His big, warm hands would cup her breasts the way he'd cupped her head while she'd cried, and his mouth would sip of her skin, indulging in the flavors of her body until she begged for mercy.

This stranger would desire her completely, seduce her thoroughly. Wash away every bit of pain, anger and self-doubt Peter had caused…and teach her everything there was to learn about physical pleasure between a man and a woman.

What a lovely fantasy.

When she opened her eyes and glanced over at Ken, she saw him watching her, his eyes wide, a tiny smile playing about his much-too-kissable lips. Another realization darted across her mind. There was no stranger from Tahoe. She'd been fantasizing about the sexy-enough-to-cry-for stranger standing right in front of her. The moments they'd spent together on the beach, the heat he'd built in her with one sweetly tender embrace and a few flirtatious words, made her wonder just what he could make her feel for a week in a resort that promised the "fulfillment of every sensual urge."

Would he come? The innuendo in her own thought

sent another rush of warmth through her body. *Oh, yes.* And so would she.

She closed her eyes again, feeling an insane pressure in her body, feeling sparks of heat shoot down her torso to pool between her legs. She was left shaking at the power of her fantasy.

"I think we should get you home," Ken said, his voice low and heavy in the silence. "You're obviously still overwhelmed."

Pamela lifted a hand to her brow, wondering how long she'd been standing there, thinking those thoughts. About him. Them. "Stop," she muttered out loud.

At least, she thought it was out loud. Or had she merely thought it? She wished she hadn't had that last drink. Her head was seriously spinning now. She was a large bundle of sensation, unable to think straight, her mind filled with images and positions she wasn't even sure were humanly possible. But, oh, how she'd love the chance to find out!

Ken's piercing eyes locked with hers. Beneath the fabric of his dress shirt, she saw his shoulders tense. He rubbed his hand against his jaw, looking uncomfortable, as if he knew what she was thinking, had heard her thoughts and was reacting to the blatant need in her.

God, had she been talking out loud?

Impossible. He was merely reacting to her obvious tipsiness. He didn't want to be stuck on a beach with a drunken, pathetic stranger! She drew in a shaky breath. "What time is it?"

"Nearly one."

"Hm...only ten hours 'til the wedding," she said, suddenly reminded that today was, indeed, her wedding day. So why couldn't she even remember her former groom's name? "My dress was very pretty."

"I'm sure you would have looked gorgeous in it," he said, still talking in that low, controlled voice that told her his mind was somewhere else.

Her shrug and heavy sigh seemed to shake him out of the mood. A gentle smile crossed his lips and he reached out to smooth a few strands of hair off her face. His fingers against her skin sent the awareness factor up another notch.

"And I'm sure you'll have another chance to wear your dress—for the right man the next time."

"Nope," she said, shrugging off the warm lethargy his touch had brought. "Won't be able to wear it."

"Why not?"

She looked at him like he was stupid. "Cause I'm gonna burn it when I get home." *Duh.*

"No, you aren't."

"Who's gonna stop me? I live alone."

"I will," he said as he took her arm to steady her on her feet. "You're in no condition to go home by yourself. I'll drive you. And while I'm there, how about I take your dress away until you're feeling better and you can decide what to do with it?"

She narrowed her eyes flirtatiously. "You're just trying to get into my apartment. Trying to get me alone."

"We're alone now," he said, a rueful laugh in his voice.

Some inner demon made her ask, "So why haven't you kissed the bride yet?"

He shook his head and made a *tsking* sound. "I try not to make a habit of kissing women who were engaged to another man two hours before. Especially not ones who've had a bit too much to drink."

"I'm not drunk," she said, aghast. "I've never been drunk in my life!"

"All the more reason why you shouldn't have drained more than four ounces of whiskey in the past hour."

"Is that why my head feels like it's three feet above my shoulders all of a sudden?"

"Could be." Ken tried to turn her toward the crossover, obviously intending to take her home.

Pamela's feet felt leaden in the sand, and the tears which hadn't fallen for the past hour or so gathered again in the corners of her eyes. "I'm such a loser. A bride who can't even get kissed on her wedding day."

Pamela wasn't feigning her sudden misery. She knew all those self-doubts, those unfulfilled desires and needs were shining clearly in her eyes. Fantasies were lovely. But they weren't going to keep her warm on her wedding night.

He must have seen her sudden sorrow. He leaned closer, touching her chin with his index finger, tilting her head up. Her breaths grew choppy and her tears dried. Pamela felt her heart pick up its pace in her chest as his lips moved toward hers. And when they met, a silent sigh rose from her body at the sense of rightness and overwhelming pleasure.

He didn't take anything she didn't offer in the kiss. When he started out gently, she sensed his restrained passion. She leaned up on her toes, fitting herself against him and sliding her arms up over his shoulders to encircle his neck. His lips were warm and firm on her own. Tasting, sipping, not invading. She tilted her head, parted her lips, deepened the kiss, knowing this one embrace would live in her memories for a very long time. It would give her something lovely to remember of this awful night.

His restraint eased, the awareness between them grew. He slid his hands down her body, tugging her tighter against him and cupping her hips. His tongue slipped into her mouth and another sigh rose from Pamela's throat. There was no frantic thrusting, no hard pulsing demands. Just sweet, languorous strokes of his tongue against hers, his lips on her mouth. She tasted him, breathed him, gave herself over to him and understood, for the first time in her adult life, what real desire was.

"Now," Ken said as he ended their kiss and took a step back, "let's get you home."

PAMELA WOKE the next day with a pounding headache, a pasty mouth that tasted like she'd eaten five bags of cotton candy, and a distinctly empty bed. "The bride might have gotten kissed, but she sure didn't get laid," she muttered as she tugged her pillow over her face to block out the morning sunlight.

She was thankful she'd made it home, at least. She vaguely remembered telling Ken where to find her spare key under a potted plant on her apartment balcony. And she remembered something about him climbing up the bannister, swinging himself over the second story railing to her patio with his powerful arms, and finding the key in the darkness. She'd been so fascinated by the flex of muscles in his arms and shoulders, the way his pants had pulled so tight across his thighs, that she'd nearly forgotten to step out of his way as he swung back down. The two of them had barely escaped falling to the ground together.

One thing she did remember was that she'd had nice dreams. Yummy dreams. Dreams about a man on a beach who'd kissed her and aroused her...then taken her home and tucked her into bed. Alone.

"A gentleman," she said with a snort, then winced as her headache intensified.

She hadn't dreamed the kiss, though. At least, she thought she hadn't! Since her head felt like someone had bounced it around a basketball court, she wasn't too sure about anything.

But, no, she couldn't possibly have dreamed anything as delicious as that kiss, that wonderful interlude with a gorgeous stranger. How many women got to experience something like that? An anonymous hour on a beach with a handsome man who truly seemed to care about her, offering her comfort and support, and a kiss that had left her almost unable to walk?

Though she probably should have been lying in bed crying about the day she was supposed to be having, she instead closed her eyes and kept thinking of him. Ken.

She didn't know his last name. But she'd memorized his face. His arms and his mouth. The crinkle in the corner of his eyes when he laughed. The hands, so big, so tender when he'd cupped her head and tenderly stroked her face while they'd kissed.

The fact that he was all she was thinking about on this her wedding day gave Pamela a shocking dose of reality. Either she was one shallow social worker, or she really hadn't loved Peter. "Good Lord, maybe I didn't," she whispered out loud, the sound of her own voice sending another shard of pain through her skull.

She'd liked the *idea* of being in love. But when it came right down to it, Peter had never made her feel, in the entire six months they were together, the way a stranger had made her feel in their single hour on the beach.

It wasn't just attraction. It was the kindness, the humor...the laughter in his eyes. She grinned, suddenly remembering the look on his face as he'd triumphantly carried her wedding gown out of her room the previous night.

She wouldn't have burned it. Really. There was a perfectly nice Goodwill shop a few blocks away.

Glancing at the clock, she saw it was noon. The afternoon reception should have been starting right about now.

The blinking red light on her answering machine caught her eye. Pamela glared at it, figuring it was a darn good thing she'd turned off the phone's ringer. She imagined it would have been ringing off the hook all morning, otherwise. A sick sense of curiosity made her push the play button. She fast-forwarded through three messages from Peter and two from her father, then turned the thing off with a shrug.

As she got up, Pamela heard a knocking coming from the front door of her apartment. Ignoring it, she headed for the bathroom and took a forty-minute shower.

Then she got ready to leave for her honeymoon.

BY SIX O'CLOCK that evening, Pamela was sitting in a window seat on a jet on the runway of Miami International Airport. She wore dark sunglasses since her head still hadn't stopped pounding, despite an afternoon filled with caffeine and aspirin. She'd ended up gathering all her luggage and leaving her apartment early in the afternoon, knowing sooner or later Peter or her father would come knocking on her door and wouldn't give up until she answered.

She had called LaVyrle and asked her friend to meet her and bring Pamela her purse. LaVyrle had demanded full details of the previous evening and had told Pamela that by the time she, Wanda and Sue had gotten up to the suite, Peter and most of the partygoers had already left.

LaVyrle, at least, understood Pamela's need to get away. "You forget about him, honey. Forget about everything here. Go be wild and be happy and deal with this mess when you get back."

After they'd parted, Pamela had spent her last bit of spare time like any bride going on a honeymoon trip. She went shopping. She hoped whatever mystery man she was going to meet and seduce in Lake Tahoe liked itty-bitty bikinis. She'd bought two of them.

Though, of course, in the cold light of day—well, the hot-June-in-Miami light of day—she didn't know if she'd be able to follow through on her grand scheme of seducing some gorgeous stranger. Last night? With that particular man? Yes, that had seemed entirely possible. Wounded feelings, raw emotions, powerful whiskey and a moonlit beach had conspired to make her think she could do that, actually have an affair with a stranger. Today she was less sure.

But, she wasn't ruling *anything* out!

Leaning back in the narrow seat on the plane, Pamela was thankful that at least she wouldn't have to make small talk with anyone. She had, after all, paid for the seat next to hers. When the flight attendant walked by, offering blankets, pillows and magazines, Pamela asked, "When do you begin beverage service?"

"Shortly into the flight," the woman said with a perky smile that grated on Pamela's nerves. "We wouldn't want anyone spilling hot coffee during take-off, now would we?"

Under her glasses, Pamela rolled her eyes. "Tell you what, the minute you start, please bring me the biggest Diet Coke you've got. And I don't mean a little plastic cupful, I want the whole can. Or a six pack." *Plus a handful of aspirin to go down with it!*

The woman's smile didn't fade. "Oh, someone's had a rough day, I can tell. I'll make sure that caffeine's on your tray table as soon as the captain gives us the all clear."

"Okay," Pamela said with a sigh. "If I'm asleep, just open up a vein and give it to me intravenously."

She hoped she'd be asleep! Since she hated flying with a passion that almost seemed like a phobia at times, she gave one silent moment of thanks for the hangover that would likely let her doze throughout most of the trip.

Pamela closed her eyes, not even watching as the flight attendant walked away to greet other passengers. She didn't realize anyone was sitting down next to her until she felt an arm brush her own.

Startled, she sat up, opened her eyes and turned. "This seat's..."

"Taken? I know. Gee, Pam, you're not in a great mood for someone leaving on their honeymoon. You almost ripped that nice little stewardess's head off."

She gasped. Him? Here? "What's going on? What are *you* doing here?"

Ken gave her an impossibly wide grin that accentuated the laugh lines around his gray eyes. "You invited me, sweetheart. Don't you remember?"

4

THE LOOK on her face nearly made this entire ridiculous situation worthwhile, Ken decided in the next few seconds. Pamela's already pale complexion went a shade closer to ghost-white. She grabbed at her sunglasses, yanking them off her nose and crunching them between shaking fingers. Leaning closer, she blinked a few times, obviously trying to ensure that it really was him. Her look of shock almost brought a laugh to his lips. Almost.

"You're insane." She shook her head slowly. "Truly. Insane."

He shrugged. How could he argue with her when he'd been telling himself exactly the same thing for the past ten hours? He'd been calling himself a complete idiot ever since he'd agreed to go on this "honeymoon" with his client's daughter.

Here he was, a successful software engineer with his own company—a company gaining an international reputation for innovation and excellence—acting as a stand-in groom. A convenient shoulder for a very gorgeous, very vulnerable woman to cry on.

Some guys probably would have been rubbing their hands together in glee. Ken just felt sick. But he'd given his word.

"You really were wasted last night, weren't you? Don't you even remember offering me the plane ticket as I was leaving your apartment?"

She sucked in her bottom lip and leaned back in her seat, looking angry and sheepish all at once. Then her eyes narrowed in suspicion. "Even if I had, you couldn't have used it. It was in Peter's name and they wouldn't have let you on without ID."

Busted!

"You're right. Frequent flyer miles."

She slumped back in her seat and he saw her wince as her head hit the rough upholstery. "Headache?"

"Somebody wake me up—I'm still asleep," she muttered, closing her eyes and shaking her head. She gave a little grimace with every movement.

Ken mentally echoed the sentiment, feeling like he was sleepwalking himself. He couldn't actually be sitting here, on an airplane, next to a woman he'd met eighteen hours ago, about to take off for a honeymoon trip to Lake Tahoe, could he? He sighed. "It's not a dream."

"Correction, it's not a *nightmare*," she retorted tartly.

A reluctant smile crossed his lips. Damn she was adorable, even when oozing headache-and-hangover-induced hostility. "That either."

"So maybe I did invite you. I'm not ruling anything out at this point," she said as she pressed her fingers into her temples. "Judging by the ferocity of the jackhammer pounding at the inside of my skull, I had a little more to drink than I should have last night. That doesn't explain why you took me up on my...invitation." She slowly opened her eyes, turned her head, and stared at him.

Ken caught her gaze, saw the beauty in the high curve of her cheek, the sweep of her dark hair against her temple. His breath caught, then he felt a smile tug at his mouth. He contemplated answering her question with a question of his own: *Which invitation was she talking about?*

Because she'd issued two invitations to him the previous night. One subtle, mumbled—expressed as a whispered fantasy involving seduction, erotic pleasure and a passionate affair with a stranger. *That* one had nearly rocked the sand on which he'd been standing. He'd felt certain she hadn't even realized she was speaking aloud, nor that he'd heard. But she *had* said it. And he had *definitely* heard it.

Kissing her after hearing those whispered, heated comments had been a *huge* mistake! Okay, so she'd looked very much in need of a kiss. Hell, if he was honest with himself, *he'd* very much needed to kiss *her* at that point. He shouldn't, however, have actually done it. His interest in Pamela Bradford had gone from a reasonable attraction to a beautiful, intelligent woman, to a raging case of hormones inspired by the feel of her slim body against his, her arms around his neck, and her mouth opening against his lips. Stepping back after only one kiss had taken every bit of willpower he owned.

"Maybe I couldn't resist?" Ken finally answered, knowing she could see the small grin he couldn't quite hide. "Maybe the mental image of you going all the way out to Reno, arriving at this Nest of Lust place and being turned away because you were alone just broke my heart."

She glared. "The Little Love Nest."

"Uh-huh. Whatever. So let's just say I didn't want you to lose out on your wedding *and* your honeymoon in the same weekend."

As she opened her mouth to argue, the stewardess began giving instructions on airplane safety. Ken, who flew so often he didn't even listen to them anymore, watched as Pamela sat up and turned to watch the flight attendant. She clutched her seatbelt and tightened it, drawing his attention down to her white-jean clad hips and long-enough-to-wrap-around-him-twice legs. That brought back all sorts of images that had raced through his head the night before after they'd kissed. Her bare thighs around his hips. On the beach, in his car, in Pamela's apartment. Hell, up against a wall.

He'd wanted her so bad his teeth hurt.

"I need a glass of water," he muttered. He swallowed hard, then forced himself to look at Miss Perky Stewardess with the too-wide-smile and the too-red lipstick. Her demonstrations with floating cushions and oxygen masks, and two-fingered pointing at the emergency exits, didn't hold his attention.

He did, however, hear Pamela muttering to herself. Noting her clenched hands on the armrest, he wondered if she was nervous about flying. "You okay?"

"Shhh!"

Ken grinned as she cast him a quelling glance, obviously annoyed that he'd distracted her from the instructions every American who'd ever flown could recite by heart. "You're cute when you're nervous," he whispered.

She was also cute when she was tipsy. And downright adorable when she was curled up in her own big, soft, bed, drifting off to sleep, as she'd been last night when she'd issued her *second* invitation to come along on this trip.

Closing his eyes, Ken thought about it, remembering the softness of her voice in the shadowy darkness of her room.

Doing anything next week? Pamela had asked with a sleepy yawn as she curled into the big bed, just about the only piece of furniture in the bedroom of her apartment. The woman lived simply, he'd noticed that as soon as he'd entered her home.

"Working," he said cautiously as he edged toward the door. He needed to get out, get away from the sight of her, tousled and vulnerable, wearing the oversize Miami Heat T-shirt she'd donned while he took her wedding gown out to his car a few minutes before. "Why?"

"Wanna come to a honeymoon with me?"

He nearly tripped over the small mountain of suitcases in the corner of her bedroom. "Excuse me?"

"They won't let me in if you don't. Honeymoon Nazis."

Ken almost chuckled at the disgruntled tone in her voice. "I'm sure they'll let you in if you've paid."

She punched her pillow, rolled over and muttered, "No groom, no room. So, take the ticket on the dresser and come, okay? You don't have to talk to me or anything, you know, just have a honeymoon."

He closed his eyes, almost laughing at his vision of what she offered. A honeymoon with no talking? A gorgeous woman, hot sex, a luxury resort and no conversation. Throw in a big-screen TV with a 24-hour sports channel, plus an unlimited supply of beer and chicken wings, and it sounded like the male version of heaven.

Only a few minor problems. He wasn't the groom. They weren't married. And no way in hell was he getting involved—delicious hot and wild sex or anything else—with a woman who'd planned to marry someone else in a few short hours!

"Sorry, sweetheart," he said before leaving the room. "Can't do it. But, hey, maybe you could ask me again in six months or so." After she'd recovered from Peter "The Slimeball" Weiss. Oh, yeah, he could definitely picture taking her up on her invitation, in one way or another, after her fiancé was well and truly out of her system.

She mumbled something unintelligible as she fell asleep. Ken stood in the doorway, the light from the living room shining in on her face. He stared at her for one more moment, then left, locking the doorknob to her apartment behind him, telling himself he'd get to know her better later. *Much* better. *Much* later.

Knocked from behind as the passenger in the next row accidentally kicked his seat, Ken forced the memory of the sleeping, innocent, sweet-faced Pamela out of his mind. Glancing over, he saw the bleary-eyed, frowning, suspicious-looking Pamela staring out the window with her nose nearly pressed against the glass. Their plane was sitting on a runway, their takeoff delayed due to the long lineup of planes waiting to depart. Pamela looked as nervous as a retail store clerk the day after Thanksgiving.

"Are you going to be okay?"

She nodded too quickly, causing her dark hair to flop down over her eyes. Not thinking about it, Ken reached over and pushed it aside, noting the silky smoothness between his fingers. His breathing slowed, and he watched as hers sped up. Her lips parted and a slow flush spread across her high cheekbones.

Her own hand rose from her armrest, moving slowly until her fingers rested lightly against his. Her eyes never breaking their stare, a slow, very gentle smile spread across her lips—the kind he'd dreamed about during his few restless hours of sleep the previous night.

He shouldn't have touched her. Shouldn't have put the kindling to the banked fire that had existed between them since the previous night when they'd kissed on the beach. Yet here he was, with his fingers tangled in her hair, touching the soft skin at her temple, breathing in the sweet lemon-tinged scent of her shampoo and hearing the tiny sigh that escaped her lips.

She continued to touch him, too. Uncertainty shone in her eyes, along with something else. Wonder at first, then heat. The fire was starting up all over again. He felt it. She felt it, too. But she didn't pull away.

"What's your last name?" she finally whispered, as if

trying to break the heady silence that had fallen between them in a few sexually charged moments.

"McBain," he said as he finally pulled his hand away. "My name's Ken McBain."

He watched, waiting for a spark of recognition, wondering if her father had ever mentioned him to her. Apparently not.

She gave a slow nod, as if coming to some great internal decision. "Yes, you can come with me, Ken McBain. I don't know why you decided to, but you can come."

She didn't know why he'd decided to? Hell, *he* had no idea what he was doing here! Any idea that this would be okay, that he could handle it, could put aside the attraction he felt for Pamela had evaporated the minute he'd touched her.

He was in serious trouble. Ken struggled to find the resolution he'd felt last night. The memory of what a stupid sucker he'd been for getting involved on the rebound with Liz, his former girlfriend, had made it easier to convince himself he'd be able to avoid allowing anything to happen between him and another heartbroken woman. But those protestations weren't going to do him a damn bit of good if he let himself get caught in the web of raging need he felt whenever any portion of his anatomy connected with any portion of Pamela Bradford's.

"I guess I haven't quite kicked off my role as protector," he finally said, noting that she waited for some kind of reply. "Not to mention I could use a vacation!"

She smiled, but her eyes still shone with confusion.

Then, resigned, she leaned back in her seat. "I need some rest."

"Go ahead. We can save the sparkling conversation for the honeymoon," Ken said. "Oh, no, I forgot. No talking, right?"

She gave him a confused look, obviously not remembering her promise from the night before.

"Forget it. Get some sleep, Pam."

Ken watched her for a moment, noting the way her long lashes brushed her pale cheeks as she tried to nap. The dark circles under her eyes could have been caused by tears, or sleeplessness. He wanted them gone. Wanted her unhappiness gone. He was going to make that happen during this trip.

She moved closer, dropped her head on his shoulder, trusting him to be her pillow. Then she moved her hand over his on the armrest. Lacing her fingers through his own, she mumbled, "Thank you, Ken."

For the first time, he was glad he'd decided to come.

That surprised him, since he'd figured there was nothing that could make him happy after he'd told her father he would do this.

The previous night, Jared Bradford had used his caller ID to track Pamela's call from Ken's phone. He hadn't wasted time asking dumb questions—like why his daughter had used Ken's phone when the two of them didn't know each other. He'd just pleaded with Ken to make sure she was okay, make sure she didn't do something dangerous or rash.

Ken hadn't been very tactful when confronting Jared about his involvement in Pamela's love life. He had, however, paused to listen to the man's explanation. Somehow, he'd found himself almost believing Jared when he said he'd never conspired with Peter Weiss. Knowing from their brief working relationship just how much he loved to talk about his stubborn but much-loved daughter, Ken thought he could see how Jared could be sucked in, thinking Peter's questions about her likes and dislikes meant he truly wanted to make her happy.

Jared certainly hoped to do whatever he could to ease Pamela's pain, going so far as to practically *insist* that Ken go with her on the trip to Lake Tahoe to make sure she was all right. Hearing Jared talk about his daughter's "innocence" Ken had begun to believe he understood why Peter had been operating under the false assumption that Pamela was, er, *inexperienced*.

Ken had refused, of course, telling Jared he felt sure Pamela would be okay. Even as he'd said the words, though, he'd questioned them. Would she? Would she really be okay? Were all those whispered, heated fantasies she'd uttered on the beach just alcohol-inspired dreams that wouldn't amount to anything?

Peter's betrayal had to have left Pamela questioning her own appeal. She'd said as much on the beach, mumbled about needing to act on the physical desires she'd suppressed during her relationship with her detached former fiancé. Would she really go find a warm, willing body to play substitute groom? To drown her misery in a spontaneous, anonymous affair that would soothe her emotions and make her feel like a desirable woman again?

Like hell she would! Not while there was breath in his body would Ken stand aside and let another man take what she broken-heartedly offered.

He didn't even try to kid himself that he was being purely self-sacrificing. Okay, maybe it was part chivalry, part loyalty to her father, even partly the thought of his own sisters. But it was also a big part self-interest.

He didn't want her getting involved with *anyone* while she got over Peter. Once she was over the bastard, Ken hoped the only man she'd be interested in getting involved with was *him*.

Selfish? Maybe. Determined? Absolutely. There had been some amazing chemistry working between them last night and he was determined they'd find out what it meant. But that wouldn't happen if she went out to Tahoe, took up with a stranger and got her heart trampled on some more. She'd likely come back swearing off men altogether!

It would be tough enough to make her understand why he'd deceived her, lied by omission about the fact that he worked with her father. Even though it was only a short-term project, in essence, her father was his boss for the next couple of months. Ken had felt more than one serious pang of guilt when he thought about that. Damn, the woman had been deceived enough!

When she found out he'd been at the party, she'd likely explode; he just hoped he could make her understand. She needed someone. She deserved to have someone looking out for her interests, making sure she was okay. And if he had to deceive her to do that, then he'd have to live with the guilt—and pay for it later when he begged her to forgive him!

So he'd said yes.

He was stepping in merely as a substitute for her dear old dad—the one she pretty much hated right now. He'd run interference between Pamela and any smooth-talking user who might spot the loneliness in her eyes and try to take advantage of her sadness. That was it. A big-brother type. Forget about their kiss. Forget about the attraction. Forget about those long legs mere inches from his own, and the sweet smell of citrus rising from her hair.

Yep, he could do it. He'd just be standing there, a solid wall between Pamela Bradford and anything even remotely resembling sex.

There would be no torrid affair. No sweet, smooth legs wrapped around anyone's hips. No hours and hours of languid kissing and stroking. No frantic thrusting into her writhing body. No warm oil massages and mirrors and...

Ken shuddered. "Forget water, I think I need a scotch."

As the plane began to move again, Pamela's eyes shot open. She became so distracted by her utter terror of flying that she nearly forgot about the man sitting next to her. Thankfully, his thick forearm, into which she was digging her fingers hard enough to make him wince, reminded her that at least he wasn't a stranger—well, not entirely, anyway.

Thrusting all confusion, humiliation and growing excitement at his presence out of her head, she concentrated on willing the wings of the plane to stay connected to its body.

As she mentally chanted the words, *Don't let me die a virgin,* she forced aside the deep-down gut belief that if man were meant to fly the whole gravity thing wouldn't have happened!

"Are you sure you're okay?" Ken asked.

Pamela darted her eyes toward him, noting his genuinely concerned expression. "I, uh, don't fly too well," she told him in a loud whisper.

"No, really?" he teased. His grin faded when she glared at him. "I'm sorry. I'm not making fun of you. But you do know that statistically there's nothing to worry about. More people die in car crashes every year than plane crashes."

She winced. "Did you have to bring up the 'c' word?"

His eyes positively twinkled. "Car?"

A tiny giggle escaped her lips, but turned into a groan as the plane picked up speed and roared down the runway.

"Don't you ever travel?"

She tilted her head toward him, but kept her eyes glued to the window. Casting quick, anxious glances between his face and the outside, where the long stretch of pavement passed beneath the wheels of the plane with growing speed, she said, "Boats."

"Boats? You travel by boat?"

She nodded. "Usually."

"You don't mind being in the ocean in a boat for days

at a time, rather than hopping on a plane and getting to where you're going in a matter of hours?"

To Pamela, there was no comparison. "Of course not."

"Remember the *Titanic?*"

She snorted. "Remember the Coast Guard?"

"Seems like a roundabout way to travel."

"My mother doesn't like to fly either," Pamela said with a shrug, finally tearing her attention away from the window to focus entirely on him. "Because once when I was a little girl we had a serious problem and an emergency landing. I remember sliding down the big rubber slide, hearing people scream, holding my mother's hand until our fingers became separated on the way down, being caught by a fireman at the bottom."

He remained silent. As they started to lift off the ground, the pressure pushed her back into her seat, and she jerked her attention to the window, wanting one more sight of land. Finally, when they were high enough that she was seeing clouds instead of treetops, she banged the window blind shut. Glancing over at Ken, she saw a look of understanding on his face.

"That must have been awful. No wonder you prefer boats."

"Mother won't fly at all. I do when I can't avoid it."

"No boats to Reno, huh?"

His sympathetic grin actually brought a smile to her lips. "Nope. And the snake didn't want to go on a cruise."

"So the Tahoe Den of Desire was worth the risk of flying?"

Pamela narrowed her eyes. "Ya know, no one said you *had* to come along on this trip!"

"But I'm here."

"And I still haven't figured out why," she said, leaning closer to him to avoid letting the flight attendant, who was passing by, hear their conversation.

His eyes, inches from hers, narrowed as he studied her face. Pamela inhaled slowly, getting lost again in the strength of his jaw, the blue-black sheen of his thick hair. And his eyes...yes, definitely a silvery-gray color that had her thinking of a newly minted coin.

Her gaze lowered to his mouth, his incredibly well-defined lips, and she remembered their kiss. Pamela slowly released the breath she'd been holding, and sucked in another between her teeth, wondering why her heart suddenly picked up its beat.

So they'd kissed. He'd held her. He'd comforted her. He'd cared for her like no one else other than her parents ever had in her life. Did it mean anything beyond the fact that he was one heck of a nice guy?

Or maybe he wasn't. Maybe he'd come for one reason—because he wanted her, too. That thought sent another rush of excitement through her body, leaving her reeling. Confusion and nervousness warred with the same thrill of pleasure she'd felt when he'd touched her face earlier.

That intensity in his eyes, the way he was clenching his fists in his lap, the coiled restraint in his tightly held body, all told of some great struggle going on within him. Was the flirtatious, smiling image merely a pretense?

"Why did you come?" she asked, her voice low and needy, demanding the truth.

She waited, wanting to hear him admit it, *needing* him to admit that he wasn't just a nice guy. He was coming to act on the unspoken invitation he'd obtained from her the night before.

She'd been wanton in his arms during their one kiss, she remembered that much. And he wanted more. Was that it? She held her breath, hoping it was the truth. Wondering if she could go through with it, this reckless, passionate affair with a man she'd known for mere hours.

When she remembered the way he'd covered her with his coat, the sweet smile on his face as he'd taken her wedding gown away, the way she'd felt in his arms, she realized the truth. Yes. Yes, she could. With him, she could.

"Tell me." *Tell me you're going to bring me to life.*

He shifted, looking uncomfortable. "I liked you last night."

She nodded, encouraging him.

"I was worried for you."

"There's got to be more to it than that." She leaned closer, so their shoulders nearly touched and her breast brushed against his arm. He looked down, a bead of sweat breaking out over his upper lip.

"I had to go out West anyway?" he offered weakly, still staring down as if he'd never seen the bright shade of pink of Pamela's shirt before in his life and had to memorize it. He shifted again, straightening his legs.

A strange sense of power shot through Pamela. He wanted her. She didn't need him to say it. His body made it clear—his labored breathing, the sheen of sweat on his brow, the tense way he held his arms. He was holding back, controlling it, but it was there. She nearly laughed with delight.

"You don't have to explain," she said. "I know how you're feeling. I've been the same way since last night."

He raised one eyebrow. "You do? You *have?*"

Pamela slid her tongue out to moisten her lips, noting that his eyes immediately shifted and he watched, very closely. She dropped her voice a bit lower. "We don't have to make excuses, don't have to justify it."

He crossed and uncrossed his legs, still looking at her mouth. "No excuses?"

Pamela shook her head and leaned closer. "We're two adults. Two mature, consenting adults."

"Uh, Pamela, listen…"

"Ken, look, we're strangers, that's obvious. But something's happened between us. The attraction is undeniable. We're on our way to spend seven days at a luxury resort that promises to indulge every sensual urge." *Where on earth had she found the nerve to say that?*

"Sensual urge?" This time his voice shook. He ran a hand across his mouth. "Pamela, I don't think…" Before he could finish his sentence, his seat was again jolted from behind. Pamela watched as he turned to peer through the crack between their seats, glaring at the elderly man behind him.

"No, don't think," she said when he turned his attention back toward her. "Neither one of us has to think about this. There's been something happening between us since the minute we met. I'm tired, Ken, so tired of letting other people decide what I'll do and when I'll do it. Lately, my career is about all I've had the energy to fight for. Somewhere along the way I started letting other people run my personal life."

First her father, then Peter. Well, no more. It was time for Pamela to take charge of her own sexual identity. And the man sitting next to her was the one she wanted to identify with!

"So let's take this moment. Spend a glorious week teaching each other how good a purely physical relationship can be between two people who want each other so badly." Her belief that she was doing the right thing carried her through the shock of saying something like that out loud to a relative stranger.

Pamela did hear the shakiness in her voice, though, and wondered if he noticed. Did he know the effort this took her? Or did he think she was some oversexed, experienced woman who was used to having casual flings? Maybe it was best to let him think that. If he knew her actual level of experience—basically none— he might turn her down.

"Well, what do you say, Ken McBain? Seven days of physical pleasure with no one to answer to and nothing to stop us except the limits of our own desire." She heard a purr in her own voice as she continued, "Are you up for it?"

She watched him swallow, hard. Glancing down, Pamela noticed the sudden tightness of his khaki trousers, which he could no longer disguise by simply shifting his legs. God, they hadn't even touched and he was magnificently *ready*. Her mouth went dry and she got hot and achy down low, deep inside. Her own jeans felt tight and wonderfully uncomfortable. Pamela knew she'd made the right decision.

"Yes, I *definitely* think you're *up* for it," she whispered.

He groaned. He literally groaned out loud. Pamela wanted to clap with delight.

Finally, Ken ran his hands through his own hair, leaned back in his seat and took a few deep breaths. "No, Pamela, no." He cleared his throat. "I like you. I'm attracted to you. I want to get to know you—but in a *platonic* sense."

She froze.

"I'm sorry," he continued, his voice growing more forceful. "But this honeymoon is going to involve absolutely *no* sex."

5

JERKING BACK, Pamela sat straight up in her seat, then stared at him. He meant it. The look on his face—kind yet resolute—told her he was serious.

For the second time in twenty-four hours, she'd basically offered herself to a man and once again she'd been left feeling rejected and humiliated. Pamela willed the tears gathering in the corners of her eyes not to fall. Glancing in panic toward the front of the plane, she noticed the Occupied sign was lit, and decided not to leap over him to escape to the tiny bathroom.

She wanted to hide her face in mortification. More than that, she wanted to call him a liar, and then hit him.

As it turned out, she didn't have to, because the elderly man in the seat behind Ken took care of that. Before Pamela realized it was happening, he'd leaned over the high-backed chair and bopped Ken on the top of the head with his rolled-up newspaper.

"Ow," Ken exclaimed, shifting to look at the other man.

The man shook his index finger toward Ken. "What are you, crazy? Are you insane? Or didja get your parts blown off in a war or something?"

Pamela, still reeling at Ken's announcement that he

would not be making love to her during their "honeymoon," found herself waiting for Ken's answer. Then she blushed as she realized the elderly gentleman with the shock of thick white hair and the bright blue eyes had been listening to their conversation.

"Could you please mind your own business?" Ken said between gritted teeth.

"Not when you're being a damned idiot." The man glowered fiercely as he stood and leaned over the back of Ken's seat. "No sex? Are ya blind? Or are ya one of those namby-pamby girlie-boys? This babe wants ta have wild sex with ya on your own honeymoon and you tell her *no?*"

A heavyset woman sitting across the aisle, who, Pamela noticed, had been pretending to read the upside-down paperback in her lap, turned with a big smile. "Honeymoon? Oh, goodness, they're newlyweds having their first lovers' quarrel! Isn't that adorable, Stu?"

A balding man with red-rimmed eyes, wearing a Hawaiian shirt and pale blue Bermuda shorts, leaned forward to look past his wife's girth. "You got it backward, son. It's the wife who says no sex whenever you get in a fight." His wife playfully smacked his hand. The husband gave Ken a long-suffering look that said, *See what you have to look forward to?*

Pamela sucked in her lip to contain a laugh as Ken's face went a dark shade of red. He muttered a curse while others on the plane began turning in their seats to look toward them.

"Don't you worry about him," the wife said as she leaned across the aisle to catch Pamela's eye. "You put on one of those pretty lacy white nightgowns I'm sure you got at your bridal shower and he'll be raring to go!"

Pamela managed a weak nod.

"And if that doesn't work," the older woman continued in a matter-of-fact tone, "try black leather."

A screech of laughter rose up in Pamela's throat, but she clamped her lips shut. Beside her, Ken's eyes went wider, and he looked around at the attention they were drawing from the entire front section of the plane.

Though it seemed things couldn't possibly get any more embarrassing, the perky flight attendant came back to up the humiliation factor another notch. "Did I hear someone say we have a honeymooning couple with us? Oh, my, is that why you were cranky when you got on board, honey? You and your new hubby had a tiff after the wedding?"

Now it was Pamela's turn to blush.

"We have complimentary bottles of champagne available. How about I get some glasses and we toast your happiness?"

"I'll toast to a man having sex on his wedding night, that's what *I'll* toast to!" the elderly man said with a belligerent thrust of his jaw.

Biting her lips didn't help. Covering her mouth didn't help either. Pamela suddenly erupted into laughter, almost snorting in hilarity as she took in the entire scene. Everyone on the plane was watching, lecturing Ken on how to be a good husband and her on whether white lace or black leather was appropriate wedding night attire. And they weren't even married!

She saw Ken's shoulders start to shake, then he was

laughing, too. He nodded at the old man as he agreed to make love to his "bride" that night, and agreed with Mrs. Red Dress that while black leather was indeed titillating, it was maybe best to keep the actual wedding night all white lace.

While the stewardess went off to fetch the free champagne, and others on the plane offered congratulations on their marriage, Pamela said under her breath, "We'll talk about the *terms* of our vacation later, okay? I know you're a wonderfully nice guy, and I somehow suspect you're trying to be chivalrous. But don't. Wait until you hear what it is I need and want before you make any decisions, okay?"

He didn't reply, didn't say no—just stared at her, weighing her words. He released a heavy breath, then glanced around, apparently to ensure no one was listening this time. "Pamela, there's no question there's something between us. Once you're over your exfiancé, maybe something will even come of it—*then*. In the meantime, we can certainly get to know each other better."

Well, at least he'd admitted the attraction! It wasn't quite the lustful declaration she wanted, but it was a start. "So you admit it. You feel the same way. You want me, too?" Hearing the hesitation in her own voice, she wondered if he knew how much his answer meant to her.

Leaning closer, Pamela tried to block the old man's view between the seats with her body. Pressing against Ken, she prodded, "It's not one-sided? You're not *pretending* you're interested?"

Her breath caught in her throat as she waited for his reply. Finally, he reached out an index finger to touch her chin and tilted her face up.

The sweet intensity in his stare shocked her. "Pamela, I want you so bad I don't know if I'm going to make it off this plane without spending a good ten minutes alone in the bathroom to, uh, *ease* the pain."

"Ease the...oh my," she whispered, realizing what he meant.

He continued with a throaty chuckle, "Like I nearly had to last night after I took you home."

She clenched her fist in her lap. "Last night?"

"Yeah, Pamela. Last night." He leaned closer, so that his lips were close enough for her to feel his exhalations against her skin. His breath smelled of mint, his cologne of the sea, and she shivered, aching with pure, undiluted need.

"Do you think it was easy for me, taking you home, walking away from you after one kiss? When what I really wanted to do was tear our clothes off, carry you into the water and make love to you while the waves pounded us both into oblivion?"

Her mouth went dry and Pamela had to clench her legs together, wondering why she'd started this torture for which she was now going to suffer. "I didn't realize..."

"You were whispering about a honeymoon and all I could see were your thighs wrapped around my hips, me buried so deep inside you that you'd scream at how good it felt."

Pamela whimpered as the sensitive flesh between her

thighs grew hotter, wetter. She wanted to cry out, to tell him to stop, that she couldn't take the sound of his voice and the look of passion on his face.

She said nothing.

"I wanted to taste every inch of you. To lick away those tiny bits of icing you had on your arms...your thighs. To put my mouth on you and watch your face as you came apart."

"Oh, please," she managed to mutter, helpless as her thigh muscles began to shudder. She pushed her clenched hands down to her lap.

"Yes, to hear you say that—please—hear you tell me you were ready for me. Then thrust into you so hard I could push every painful memory of that bastard you were engaged to right out of your brain, Pamela."

Someone passed by in the aisle, heading toward the front of the plane, and Ken suddenly seemed to realize what he was saying. He muttered a curse and pulled back. "I'm sorry."

"Don't be," she said hoarsely once she was able to draw enough breath into her lungs to be able to speak. "You can't know how much I *needed* to hear that."

"Yeah, well, I didn't mean to say it."

The raging hormones practically rolled off him; Pamela could feel his desire coming toward her in heat-laden waves of energy. Her body arched closer to him, still quivering.

What on earth could this man make her feel if he actually *touched* her? Considering she'd come close to having a screaming orgasm on a crowded plane just at the sound of his voice, she had a feeling actually making love to him would be beyond the realm of her imagination.

"I came on this trip with you certain that I could control the way I feel when we're together." He shook his head, obviously still angry with himself. "I'm not some teenage kid—I can enjoy getting to know a woman without having to take her to bed right away."

She paused for a heartbeat. "What if that's what she wants you to do?"

He met her stare evenly. "Then she's going to be disappointed. That's not why I'm here."

"Yeah, I've got it," she muttered. "You're here strictly to be my friend, Mr. Protector."

"Don't make me out to be some white knight, sweetheart. I have my own motives."

She tensed, waiting for the other shoe to drop, knowing all about men with their own hidden agendas. "Motives?"

"I've said I'm not going to get involved with you while you're suffering a broken heart over your ex. But I'm also here to make damn sure no one else does either."

Not understanding at first, she lifted a brow.

"No other man is going to see that look in your eyes and give you what you've been begging for since we met last night." His tone was confident, verging on arrogant. "I'm the only man who's going to give you that, Pamela—when you're ready, not before. Then I'll make you forget Peter ever existed."

Another wave of excitement rolled through her at the certainty in his voice. "Promise?"

He nodded slowly, a small smile on his lips, utter confidence in his stare. His intensity spoke of heat. Passion. Everything she wanted—not later—now.

"I promise," he finally said. "Will you promise me something?"

"I'll try."

"Give it time, Pamela. Let it happen naturally. Take this chance for your heart to heal. I'll be there to make sure you don't do anything you'll regret in the future, like any friend would."

"Friend?"

"That's all I'm offering right now, Pamela. That's all I'm willing to be. Can you live with that?"

Could she? Be merely a friend to this tender, charming, sexy-as-pure-undiluted-sin man? He'd made her laugh, made her nearly have a shattering orgasm in the middle of a crowded plane, and was fighting his intense attraction to her for *her* own good. Could she give up any more heated, whispered words? Kisses like the one that had rocked her world the night before?

Not bloody likely.

"You can be my friend, Ken," she said with a gentle smile. She saw his tension ease. "And I can do my damnedest to change your mind."

Before he could reply, the flight attendant returned, carrying the free minibottle of champagne. Shooting Pamela a look that promised their conversation would continue later, Ken poured them each a serving while everyone watched. Lifting his glass, Ken looked around at other couples in nearby rows and said, "Here's to all successful marriages, and to a happy, fun-filled honey-moon."

Pamela caught his eye, heard the unspoken message in his toast. Happy? Fun-filled? In other words, pla-tonic.

Uh-uh. No way, mister. No way.

"I have a toast of my own," she said, lifting her glass again. "To white lace *and* black leather—both of which I happen to have in my suitcase."

KEN WONDERED how long it would take for the oxygen to be sucked out of his lungs if he leapt out of the plane somewhere over the northern part of Florida. Would he freeze to death or suffocate first? It didn't matter, he supposed, even if he survived screaming all the way down to the ground. Anything seemed preferable to sit-ting here with a record-setting hard-on while all around him people laughed and toasted his marriage to the bright-eyed temptress in the seat next to him.

White lace. Black leather.

"God help me."

He mumbled several silent prayers for mercy over the next few hours while they proceeded across the country on what he was now calling "the honeymoon-from-hell plane." It seemed everyone on board, includ-ing the pilot, felt the need to congratulate them...and to comment on their "lovers' tiff" during the flight.

One young man with a pierced nose and long dirty-blond hair swept back into a ponytail, offered to lend them his copy of the *Kama Sutra*. Ken somehow man-aged to refrain from asking him why he felt the need to travel with a text on the Hindu art of lovemaking. Pamela had no such forbearance. The young man spent several minutes happily explaining why he worshipped women and wanted to do anything to please them.

The young man's lighthearted flirtation with Pamela made her smile, so Ken allowed it. Briefly. He didn't consider himself a caveman type, and Pamela definitely needed a shot of confidence after the night she'd had with her fiancé. Besides, they weren't *really* a newly married couple going on their honeymoon. He didn't have any claim on Pamela. And there wasn't much the blond stud could do on a crowded plane. Still, Ken felt a strong urge to knock Mr. *Kama Sutra* to the back of the plane when he started talking to Pamela about his *lingam*.

When she reached out to accept the book the young man offered, leaning farther out toward the aisle, she again pressed her breasts into his upper arm. Ken gritted his teeth.

"I'm sure this'll be fascinating," she told the man.

Ken only caught a glimpse of the cover but instantly recognized that it did, indeed, contain the ancient Hindu sexual teachings. He held his hand out, blocking her from taking it, and stared at the blond young man. "If you value your *lingam*, I suggest you go back to your seat," he said, knowing he probably sounded like a jealous moron, and not giving a rat's ass.

The other man nodded. "Okay. No harm, no foul."

After he left, the old man behind him cleared his throat and muttered, "'Bout time."

"What's a *lingam?*" the woman in the red dress asked her husband. He didn't seem to know; Ken did not offer any answers. He was not at all inclined to start discussing the male sex organ with strangers. Not when *his* was causing him such excruciating discomfort every time Pamela touched his thigh as she leaned over to talk to the other couple, or whispered into his ear, or let her soft hair brush against his cheek. When Pamela got up to use the restroom, insisting that he remain seated while she wiggled her sweet, jean-clad backside right in front of him in order to exit the row, he hissed.

She heard, took no mercy, leaned close and whispered, "Wanna join the mile-high club?"

"Pamela..." he warned.

She grinned, then, instead of walking toward the bathroom, sat in the vacant aisle seat next to him. "I know this flight hasn't been pleasant for you. You've been a very good sport."

"Oh, yeah, I so enjoy looking like some kind of modern-day eunuch who won't have sex with a gorgeous woman," he muttered.

She kissed his cheek, whispered in his ear, "I know the truth. Thank you for admitting you want me, even though it made for a rather, er, uncomfortable plane ride."

Ken tried to focus on the sincerity of her words, and to ignore the softness of her hair against his face and the curve of her lips just inches from his own.

"Remember, it's completely mutual, okay?" she continued, her eyes holding a look of tender understanding. "I feel everything you're feeling. And whenever you're ready to shrug off your protector jacket and see that I am a grown-up woman making grown-up decisions, you can help me put us *both* out of our misery."

He started breathing again about sixty seconds after she slipped away, then whispered, "Will this flight never end?"

IT DID, of course, finally end, and by that point Pamela was on a first-name basis with the old man behind them and the couple in the seats across the aisle. Mrs. Red Dress seemed to enjoy instructing Pamela on wifely duties from the other side of the plane. Her harried hubby Stu rolled his eyes so often Ken was surprised they didn't get stuck up inside his head.

She charmed them all. Her quick smile, genuine laugh and the twinkle in her brown eyes charmed him as well.

Though deadly when she was flirting with him, he found her even more disconcerting during their long, casual conversations throughout the flight. She talked about her job and her dreams, about her past and her relationship with her parents.

They debated politics and sports. She told him she could whup his butt in a game of hoops and he suspected she could, particularly after learning that she'd been courted by the WNBA during her college years.

He liked her. Truly enjoyed her company. That, combined with the physical attraction he'd felt for the woman since the first time he'd seen her, made the guilt factor even worse. He was lying to this wonderfully down-to-earth, charming, beautiful woman—a woman he probably could go nuts over given half a chance.

He wouldn't be given half a chance, however, if he couldn't make her understand why he hadn't told her who he really was.

When they landed in Reno, Ken was up, pulling his carry-on from the overhead compartment, before the plane even came to a complete stop. That earned him a frown from the flight attendant, who was not so perky after five hours in the air, and a nod of approval from the old geezer, who seemed to take Ken's anxiousness as a sign that he couldn't wait to be alone with his new bride.

"Are you ready to go, Pamela?" he asked as she continued chatting with others onboard, making no move to exit.

"Oh, he's so anxious," one of the older ladies in the front section of the plane said with a sigh. "Isn't that sweet?"

As they left the plane, Ken paused every few feet to accept congratulations, noting the happiness on Pamela's face. Remembering the tears he'd seen in her eyes the night before, he acknowledged that the humiliating plane ride was worth one of her bright smiles.

Her mood had definitely improved after he'd been stupid enough to confess how badly he wanted her. Ken realized he'd made a very serious tactical mistake. Her femininity had been rocked by her fiancé; now he'd practically tossed a gauntlet at her feet, almost challenging her to make him act on the attraction between them. Telling her he wouldn't had been a line drawn in the sand. She'd already begun to cross it. He didn't know if he had the strength to draw another one.

As soon as they got to the spa, and had some privacy, they were going to have to have another serious talk. No way was he sticking around if Pamela had made it her mission to seduce him.

Ken wasn't stupid. It wouldn't take much effort at all and would be breaking his rules against getting involved with a woman on the rebound, and taking advantage of a woman who was hurting and vulnerable. So, he'd need to lay down some ground rules for this vacation. Number one, no white lace. Numbers two through ten, no black leather. Numbers eleven through twenty forbade the heated looks, sultry glances and all those innocent touches she'd managed to torture him with during the flight.

They'd just have to move past the sexual tension so thick between them he could spread it on toast, and try to enjoy their vacation like any two strangers in a honeymoon resort would.

How tough could that be? They'd be at an exclusive hotel with lots of things to do. There'd probably be horseback riding, kayaking, lots of activities that did not involve giving in to his overwhelming urge to throw her onto the nearest flat surface and take her in every way humans had ever discovered—and then some.

As the old man from the plane followed them to the gate, muttering wedding night instructions under his breath, Ken sighed in resignation. Pamela, who'd looped her arm in his, leaned close to whisper, "Almost over. We'll be another anonymous vacationing couple in a few minutes."

"Thank goodness."

He took one or two more steps, not noticing at first when Pamela stopped moving. Glancing over his shoulder at her, he saw the color draining from her face. Her mouth hung open and her eyes were wide.

"No. Please, nothing else," he muttered out loud, almost afraid to turn and see what had sparked her reaction. Had Peter come to find her? Or was it her father?

Resigned, he followed her stare, searching for a familiar face. His gaze at first moved right past the burly, gray-haired man who wore a pale blue tuxedo and held a huge horseshoe of red, pink and white roses over his shoulders. Then he caught sight of the banner the man was carrying. It was almost enough to make a grown man cry.

Pamela somehow managed to avoid giving in to her first impulse, which was to run in the other direction and hide, and her second impulse, which was to burst into hysterical laughter. Instead, she tugged Ken behind her, and marched up to the flower-bearing man holding the banner that said, The Little Love Nest Welcomes Newlyweds Pamela & Peter!

"We're here."

A huge smile spread across the man's face. She wondered how much he'd paid for all the gold caps.

"Ah, the happy couple has arrived!" he boomed, drawing the attention of everyone nearby. "On behalfa da Little Love Nest, welcome ta Reno."

If there had been cameras around, Pamela would

have sworn someone was filming a Godfather-type movie. Because this guy was like every cinema image of a mafia enforcer she'd ever seen. His gray hair was cropped close into a blunt crew cut that hugged his square head. Though a genuine smile creased his lips, Pamela saw that his friendly blue eyes glanced in every direction, as if watching for a hit man...or a Fed. The only thing that would have completed the image would have been a black Italian suit. Somehow, his pale blue tuxedo and ruffled shirt—fresh from a 1970s prom night—didn't fit the mafia image. "Thank you so much for the welcome," she finally managed to say.

"My name's Al, and it's my pleasure. These would be for you," he said as he took the horseshoe of roses off his own shoulders. "Better let hubby carry them, though." He hung the roses over Ken's shoulders, obviously not noticing the way Ken's jaw tightened.

"Let's go get yer bags, then we'll be on our way. We got about an hour's drive, across the state line, to the southwest shore of the lake."

"Giddyap," Ken muttered between clenched teeth as Al walked away. "Looks like I won the Derby."

Pamela couldn't resist. "And you haven't even *ridden*—not yet, anyway."

His eyes narrowed at her suggestive taunt. "I think I forgot my spurs. Guess that's okay...I won't be doing any riding on this vacation anyway."

She heard the challenge and responded to it. "I might have something in my suitcase you could borrow... black leather, metal—oh, no, that'd be the handcuffs."

She watched him swallow, hard. Then he obviously shook off the sexual image and gave her a knowing look. "Don't tell me Peter was the kinky type."

"I have no idea, remember?"

Ken nodded in male satisfaction. "Oh, yeah, that's right. I remember now."

He looked too pleased with himself. Could he really be glad, for his own sake, that she hadn't consummated her relationship with Peter? Out of what? A sense of protectiveness? Or jealousy?

She hoped it was the latter.

"Hm, I just hope you're a distance rider," she finally continued, unwilling to let him have the last word, "not one of those jockeys who finishes the race in under a minute."

"It's not the speed of the race that counts," he said, his voice low and confident. "It's all in the technique."

"And not falling off the horse," she said with a grin as she turned to follow Al toward the baggage claim.

Ken fell into step beside her and gave her a look of wounded male pride. "I've never fallen off."

"Never been thrown, either?"

"No way."

"Not even if the mount was particularly, um, aggressive in her movements during the race?"

He paused, taking her arm. "That makes the ride more exciting." He leaned closer, ignoring the passengers who continued to walk by them in the terminal. "Two bodies moving together like one, pure instinct taking over as they strive toward the finish line, reaching for that big payoff."

Now it was Pamela's turn to swallow hard. She almost regretted taunting him. "Big payoff?"

"Oh, yeah," he said, his voice silky, his eyes now a dark gray as he held her gaze. "Straining toward it, going for it with every bit of physical energy they possess, then reaching that final moment when they cry out with triumph."

Her mouth dry, Pamela muttered weakly, "Sounds like you've had a lot of experience."

"Some. And believe me," he continued, his voice as seductive as a caress, "nothing feels as good as being deep *inside* that winner's circle, achieving the *ultimate* prize."

"Oh, good grief, you did it again," she muttered as her legs weakened beneath her. She shuddered, rubbed a hand over her eyes and shook her head. When she looked at him again, Ken was watching, a knowing smile playing about his lips.

"Do you know what you're doing to me? Right here, in the middle of a public airport? Jeez, you ought to register that voice of yours as a lethal weapon."

"Don't start playing sexy word games with me, sweetheart, unless you expect me to play along."

"Well, heck," she said in confusion, "isn't that the problem? You not wanting to play along?"

"Don't ever think it's a question of wanting or not, Pamela. There's no doubt about what I want." He lifted his hand and brushed his fingers against her cheek, burning her, making her ache even more. "It's all about the timing."

He turned to catch up to the driver and Pamela fell

into step behind him. Noting the amused looks he was getting from passersby, she had to give him credit for not pitching the flowers into the nearest trash can. Al, the driver, who'd apparently just noticed that they hadn't immediately followed him, waited for them to catch up. When they reached his side, he gave them a rundown on the weather and local activities, most of which seemed to involve gambling. He appeared to be an expert in that area.

When they reached the baggage claim area, Al asked them for a description of their bags, then left to retrieve them. As soon as he was out of earshot, Ken asked, "Exactly how much do you know about this resort, Pamela?"

She shot him a worried glance. "Their brochures were nice."

"Do you actually know anyone who's ever stayed there?"

Biting her lip, she shook her head. "I'm sure it'll be okay, though. This area's very exclusive. Maybe the resort has some liberal hiring policies?"

They stared as Al reached for one of Pamela's bags, elbowing everyone else waiting near the conveyor out of his way. Ken winced. "Or maybe they support the local work release program!"

She didn't reply.

Al rejoined them, pushing a cart loaded with Pamela's bags and one unfamiliar one, which she assumed was Ken's. "Okay, we're all set." Giving them another toothy grin, he grabbed the flowers, draped them over the top of the suitcases on the cart and led them toward the exit. Everyone waiting in the baggage claim area stepped out of his way.

Outside, the air was damp with a recent rain. Low-hanging, murky clouds hid any sign of stars in the night sky. Pamela's internal clock forced her to emit a huge yawn. Though it was only about nine here, her body thought it was midnight. She was more than ready for a good night's sleep. Tomorrow, she decided, would be soon enough to begin the *real* honeymoon.

Now, after twice experiencing his verbal powers of seduction, she had to wonder what Ken was capable of with his hands, his lips, his...oh, how she wanted to find out!

He'd definitely paid her back for teasing him throughout the flight. Glancing at him as they walked, she hid a smile as she remembered his discomfort on the plane. He'd been positively oozing restrained sexual need! She'd done what she could to push every lustful button he had. Maybe not fair, given his insistence on a platonic honeymoon, but she didn't really care about fair right now. Peter certainly hadn't been fair with her, nor had her father. So maybe it was time for Pamela to be the taker, to get what she wanted.

And, oh, she so very badly wanted Ken McBain.

Since Pamela wasn't, by nature, a selfish person, she'd felt more than one moment's concern about using him to soothe her own heartbreak and self-doubt. When she thought about it, however, she acknowledged the truth: she didn't want him because of what had happened with Peter, nor because of the fact that she'd

never made love with anyone and feared being the
world's oldest living virgin.

She wanted him because of that smile. Those eyes.
Those hands that had held her so tenderly while she'd
cried. She wanted him because of that kiss. The feel of
his lips on hers, the sweep of his tongue in her mouth
that had stolen her breath, her will and her self-control.
She wanted him because of his laugh. Because of his
sense of humor. Because of the way he looked in his
pants...

She wanted him because he had covered her with his
jacket. Because he could make her thighs weak with a
single heavy-lidded look. And, oh, heavens yes, because of the way his whispered words had made her
lose control, had filled her mind with images she'd only
ever dreamed about—and some she hadn't.

Mainly she wanted him because she knew she would
wonder for the rest of her life what might have been if
she didn't take a chance and fully experience the joy she
felt sure she could find with him. Physically. Emotionally. In every way possible.

Okay, they hadn't met under ideal conditions. But the
sparks firing between them would have happened no
matter where they'd met. She knew it.

She also knew, without question, that he wanted her
as much as she wanted him. He'd admitted it. So he'd
decided to be chivalrous, act the part of protector? She
admired him for the gesture. But chivalry wasn't what
she needed from him.

She needed passion, soul-stirring desire and physical
fulfillment. She needed to laugh with him some more,

to make his silvery eyes darken to gray when he looked at her. Needed to kiss him senseless, as he'd done to her the night before on the beach. She needed to know him, to memorize his smell and the way his skin tasted after a shower. Needed to know what sounds he made when he made love. Needed to look into his eyes, be mentally connected with him as he exploded inside her when they finally came together.

Yes, those would be her terms for their vacation.

Pamela smiled, casting another look at him as they walked outside on the still-wet pavement. She looked forward to bringing him around to her way of thinking, knowing he might not be easy to persuade. He'd adopted the mantle of protector and it might take some serious persuasion to get him to change his mind.

Persuasion? *Seduction!*

A strong sense of purpose—and anticipation of the payoff—overcame any question in her mind that she could do it. Maybe Peter hadn't wanted her enough, but that was because his greed had been interfering with his libido.

Ken was nothing like Peter. He was honest, for one thing. He had no idea who she was, who her father was. And while he fought valiantly to suppress it, he felt the same physical draw toward her that she felt toward him.

Yes, seduction could work. Pamela suddenly found herself very thankful for those bikinis she'd bought in Miami earlier in the day—not to mention some of the other surprises LaVyrle had given her at her bridal shower. She hadn't been joking about the handcuffs!

"Oh, God, please tell me there's a Mary Kay convention in town," she heard Ken mutter. Startled out of her very pleasant musings, she followed his horrified stare.

They had reached a loop with spaces reserved for buses and limousines. The spots were full, for the most part, with tourists boarding shuttles to the various casino hotels in Reno, or to the Lake Tahoe resorts. One car stood out.

"It's pink," Ken said.

"Very," she agreed.

Her faint hope that Al would pass right by the bright pink boat parked in one of the spaces near the end of the row was quickly dashed. He cut between the nightmare and a lovely black Mercedes limousine and tossed their luggage into the trunk of the cotton-candy-mobile. He then unceremoniously dumped the flowers on top of them and slammed down the lid. "Hop in, folks!"

Ken didn't think he'd ever entered a car faster in his life. Giving a quick glance around, and noting that no one appeared to be looking in their direction, he yanked the back door open, pushed Pamela into the back seat, and dove in after her. Maybe no one had seen. *Please, let no one have seen!*

Al got into the front seat and turned to face them. "There's champagne in the fridge. Remember, we've got a whole hour until we get to the resort." He gave them a somewhat lascivious smile. "I'll give you two lovebirds some privacy. The windows are impossible to see through...and that includes this one." He pushed a button and a solid black sheet of glass slid up from behind the front seat. Before Al's face completely disappeared, he gave Ken a very obvious wink.

Then they were alone. In the semidark. Cocooned from everyone else in the entire world. For the next sixty minutes.

Pamela sat so close to him that her body touched his from knee to hip. He moved away, toward the door, trying to ignore her sweet scent and the memory of what those long legs had looked like last night on the beach—trying to forget their conversations, both on the plane and in the airport, when he'd been foolish enough to let her hear his need for her.

She scooted closer until they were touching again. *Uh-oh.*

Al's voice interrupted from an overhead speaker. "How about some music, folks?"

Thankful for the distraction, Ken nodded, then remembered Al couldn't see him. "Yes, music," he ordered. "Anything." *A marching brass band, a rap song— just nothing low and sultry!*

Then he heard the music start and knew his wish had not been granted. Donna Summer's voice, moaning orgasmic oohs and aahs as she sang "Love To Love You Baby," slid out of the stereo speakers and completed the atmosphere of raw sexual tension.

Feeling his self-control skid away in huge chunks, Ken muttered, "It's a conspiracy!"

6

"WHAT IS?" Pamela asked.

Ken looked at her out of the corner of his eye, knowing she knew what he was talking about. The innocent expression on her face couldn't hide that her body was moving...just barely...to the sexual sounds. Every gesture was a blatant invitation, designed to be impossible to refuse.

"Forget it," he muttered, trying again to move away, gain some distance. "I guess the 1970s disco music works as well as everything else has so far."

She reached into the ice bucket sitting atop the small refrigerator and glanced at the champagne bottle. "Looks like they have good taste in champagne at least." Then she slid across the roomy leather seat until her hip once again came in contact with his. "Want some?"

His mouth went dry. "Uh, is there any bottled water?"

She leaned over to open the fridge, her pink shirt pulling free of the waistband of her jeans. Ken stared at the long, pale strip of skin, the indentation of her bare waist revealed below her shirt. His gut clenched.

It took her forever to root around in the tiny refrigerator, particularly since she insisted on wiggling lower, pushing her sweet rear end against his thigh.

Conspiracy.

She finally sat up and shook her head. "'Fraid not."

He gave a helpless shrug, wondering if she knew how the soft lighting emanating from the amber bulbs in each door cast hints of gold on her hair.

Did she also know she was killing him? Could she imagine the restraint it was taking to avoid accepting the invitation at her every move? Did she know how much he wanted to press her back onto the long leather seat and explore every bit of her?

He waited, noting the sparkle in her eyes and the curve of her lips. Pamela handed him two fluted glasses that had been sitting on top of the bar, then held up the bottle of champagne.

When he reached to take the bottle from her, she waved his hand aside, popping the cork herself. Some of the pale golden fluid spurted out of the top, bubbling down over Pamela's hand. He heard her gasp, then watched as she drew the bottle toward her mouth, to lick away the moisture from her own skin.

"Lovely," she whispered throatily as she tasted the champagne. The smooth, unhurried strokes of her pink tongue on her long fingers nearly had Ken begging for mercy... *Which was what she'd intended.*

He saw the mischief in her tiny grin, combined with a look of physical pleasure. She was enjoying the sensuality of the moment—the darkness, their closeness, the music, the taste of the liquid on her own flesh. Pamela

Bradford was reveling in sensation. That gave him another insight into her character.

But her provocative teasing ended when she saw what he was certain was an explosion of answering heat in his own eyes.

"Let me," Ken murmured, not knowing where the words came from, only knowing he had to taste her or go mad. He pulled the bottle free of her hand and set it in an ice bucket on the bar, then tugged her fingers toward his lips.

Excitement widened her eyes and Ken never let their stare break. He moved closer, until his mouth was a breath away from her fingers. Only after her hand shook in his own did he slide his lips over the tip of her pinky.

She moaned, rose off the seat.

Ken moved his mouth down her finger, licking off the sweetness, tasting her with his tongue and his teeth. When he'd licked off every bit of moisture from that finger, he released it and moved to the next, taking his time, dipping his tongue to taste the tender flesh between.

"Ken…" she said on a sigh, her voice holding both an invitation and a plea.

Her hands weren't enough. He wanted to kiss every inch of her—every delectable, sweet-flavored inch.

Her mouth, however, would do for a start.

He caught her lips with his, hearing her soft groan as she parted them invitingly. He felt her hands slide behind his neck as she tilted her head to the side to deepen the kiss.

She tasted sweet, warm, her tongue meeting every stroke of his own until they were both moving to the same rhythm.

"Got to touch you," he muttered, telling himself it was crazy but unable to stop. "I have to touch you, Pamela."

She pressed closer, arching her back and sliding lower into the leather seat. He moved over her, covering her body with his own. Moving his hands to tangle in her hair, he cupped her head and continued to kiss her, deeply, endlessly, losing himself in her completely.

Then, unable to resist, he slid his hands lower, caressing her neck, her shoulders, the pale curve of her throat, her high, lovely breasts.

"Oh, please," she said, her hips jerking in reaction as he passed his flattened hands over the front of her pink cotton shirt. He felt her rock-hard nipples beneath the fabric and simply had to bend lower to taste them, making her shirt wet and warm as he sucked one tender tip into his mouth.

His hands were tugging her pink top up before his mind even had a chance to order him to stop. Her skin was hot, throbbing and vibrant beneath his fingers. He drew the shirt up slowly, peeling the tight fabric off inch by agonizing inch, relishing each strip of flesh as it was revealed.

She lifted her arms above her head, and he tossed her shirt aside. Ken heard her cry out as he moved lower to press a hot kiss on her stomach, and he paused, savoring her sweet fragrance, taking tiny tastes of her, sliding his mouth lower until he was breathing onto the front of her white jeans.

"Ken," she muttered hoarsely, "please..."

"Please what? Please relieve the pressure?" He moved back up her body, knowing the way she twisted beneath him that she'd wanted him to stay where he was. "Or should I let you suffer the way you made me suffer on that plane?"

"I need, can't...*please!*"

He moved higher, until his mouth was scraping the lace of her bra. His breathing grew ragged as her nipples puckered and hardened beneath the white lace. He nudged one strap off her arm, kissing a path along the high curve of one breast. When he slid his tongue beneath the fabric for just a taste, a simple taste of her sweet skin, she jerked so hard they nearly flipped off the seat.

"You like that."

"That's going to kill me," she muttered hoarsely. "Don't you dare stop."

Stop? Hell, he'd sooner stop drawing breath.

Finally he pulled the bra down, cupping her breast with his hand, teasing her sensitive nipple with his fingers. She grabbed his hair, pulled him closer, demanding more. When he sucked her nipple deep into his mouth, she cried out beneath him.

She was writhing now, moving wildly on the seat. Her flushed cheeks, thrashing head and audible cries told him that, incredible as it seemed, she was close to finding her ultimate release with nothing more than a few kisses and caresses.

"Please, please," she cried out, arching into him, thrusting her pelvis up against him, rubbing herself against his raging erection until his frenzy nearly matched hers. "I can't, I've never..."

She'd never had hot pounding sex in the back of a limousine? Never driven a man so out of his mind that he'd abandon all good intentions and come close to pulling her clothes off and thrusting into her now, *right now*, heedless of the driver in the front seat?

He wasn't quite that lost. But no way could he pull back. No way could he take her that far and not see her go right over the edge of the cliff. "Go with it, sweetheart, go ahead and fall. I'm right here," he muttered hoarsely.

Keeping up the heated kisses to her breasts, he moved one hand down her body in a smooth stroke until he reached her hip. Then lower, circling her thigh.

When he cupped her sex he found her jeans hot, the fabric damp. She squirmed against him, "Yes, oh, please," and jerked up harder, forcing herself against his palm.

He stroked. Once, twice. Moving up to catch her cries with his lips, he kissed her deeply but never stopped touching her, using his hand to bring her higher. Until, finally, beautifully, she cried out his name and came apart right before his eyes.

PAMELA COULDN'T MOVE. Though she imagined she made quite an interesting picture, she couldn't even bring herself to care.

She lay there beneath him, wrapped around him, trying to control her ragged breathing. He was having the same problem. Even over the sound of Marvin Gaye's voice singing about "Sexual Healing" through the car stereo speakers she could hear Ken's choppy breaths.

Lying with him, legs splayed, weak and trembling, one bare breast just inches from his mouth, she tried to come to terms with what had happened. Her entire body was sensitized, throbbing with pure electric energy. She felt something like wonder as she realized it was true—for the first time in her life, a man had brought her to orgasm.

It wasn't that she was a complete stranger to orgasms. She'd made friends with her Shower Massage at a young age, just like many other young women with inexperienced boyfriends who never knew exactly where to touch. Not that she'd usually even dated guys long enough to let them progress to any real touching!

But she'd never experienced more than that, never shared the amazing body-rocking sensations with anyone else. Until now. Him.

She couldn't imagine what it was going to be like when they went beyond touching. Though she still quivered from the aftereffects, still shook with the intensity of the pleasure he'd given her, she wanted more. She wanted him buried deep inside her.

Finally able to move, she shifted slightly, tugging him with her. "I think you almost fell off that time," she said, not trying to hide a laugh.

"Slippery seats," he muttered against her neck.

When she slipped one of her thighs between his legs, she found him rock hard against her. "Oh, my."

"Don't move," he bit out. "Just don't move."

She heard something akin to pain in his voice. "Why did you stop?" she asked, knowing the effort it must have taken him to bring her to release without finding any for himself.

"Why did I start?"

"Don't. Please don't apologize; don't try to take it back. I know all about your noble ideas, know you didn't plan to let anything happen between us. But I'm glad. I confess it. Does that make me wicked? A bad person? That I can be glad I'm here with you, like this, feeling these things I've never felt before, when I was supposed to marry someone else this morning?"

He pressed a kiss on her temple, smoothed her hair away from her brow. "You're not a bad person, Pamela. But you're very, very vulnerable. You needed someone to make you feel better and tonight that someone was me."

"*Someone?*" She stiffened beneath him. Was he saying anyone would have done as well? Suddenly angry, Pamela pushed at his chest, slipping out from under him. "That's bullshit," she muttered as she tugged her bra back up, covering her still-sensitive breast.

He sat up, eyeing her warily. Either he was shocked by her language—which she doubted—or he'd noticed the fire of anger in her eyes. "Is that what you think? That I would have let any guy with good hands and a sweet mouth make me feel what you just made me feel?"

"I didn't mean it like that," he said, his tone reasonable, which made her madder.

"Well, how did you mean it then? Do you think I'm so desperate I would've picked up someone on the plane, or Al there in the front seat, just to get my jollies and make me feel better about myself after what Peter did?"

He didn't reply for a moment, and Pamela pushed away from him, hard, shoving at his chest and sliding across the smooth leather seat. She yanked her shirt on over her head, then reached to turn down the speaker, which had moved past Motown and was now playing Madonna's "Like A Virgin."

"Look, last night you were talking about coming out here and finding some stranger to indulge in an affair with."

"You heard that?" she asked in a weak whisper.

He nodded. "All of it."

"Oh." She pushed her hair off her face, trying to deal with all the emotions still coursing through her. "And you believed it to the point that you felt the need to come with me and make sure I didn't go through with it?"

"Something like that," he admitted.

He'd said as much on the plane; it made sense now. "So you are here to stop me from having sex altogether?"

"Right."

"Including with you," she said, hearing the skepticism in her own voice.

"That's the plan."

She thought about it, tilted the tip of her index finger

against her lips, then looked at him out of the corner of her eye. "You'd better keep your day job."

He raised an inquisitive eyebrow.

"I don't think you'd make much of a living making plans for anybody. Because you suck at sticking to them."

"Pamela..."

"Hey, I'm not complaining. You've definitely made this ride more interesting. But if you think that's going to make me forget my idea of a sensual honeymoon with a sexy-enough-to-die-for stranger, you're dead wrong."

He stiffened, leaned closer and said, "Forget it, Pamela. No way in hell are you going to pick up some guy at this resort and shack up with him for a week."

He'd misunderstood. Pamela debated being honest with him. Should she admit she had absolutely no intention of shacking up with anyone but *him* for the next week? By kissing her the way he had, bringing her to the ultimate level of fulfillment without doing much more than touching her, he'd only fueled her certainty. They were going to go all the way to the end of this sexual roller-coaster ride they'd been on since last night. No question about it.

"You going to stop me?" she finally said, hearing the challenge in her tone.

"You bet your sweet ass I am."

"That might take some maneuvering that you're not quite prepared for. It might require some sacrifice on your part."

"Sacrifice?"

She nodded, meeting his eyes, noting his confusion, knowing he never saw it coming. "If you want to make sure I don't end up in someone else's bed...you might just have to keep me in yours."

KEN SOMEHOW MANAGED to avoid either strangling or jumping on Pamela again during the remainder of the drive to the resort. It took a lot of self-control—which really had long since dissipated—to ignore the sultry invitation in her smile. She flirted, cajoled and silently seduced him with each heavy-lidded glance.

He tried talking to her, insisting that she was raw from her breakup, didn't know what she wanted yet. She shrugged and said nothing. But her knowing looks told him she knew he would never be able to *not* make love to her before another day or two had passed.

He also knew she was goading him with her "affair with a stranger" plan. She wouldn't have gone through with it. Okay, he hadn't known her long, but he felt certain he knew her well. She wouldn't have been able to pick up some guy, have mindless sex and then walk away. So her threat—and outrageous solution that he keep her in his bed—had been unnecessary...but definitely effective.

She'd set her sights on him. She wanted him with an intensity matched only by the depth of his desire for her.

Damn, this was getting complicated!

He could only hope that when they arrived at the resort and were surrounded by other people and lots of activities, they'd be able to dilute the sexual tension still raging between them. There had to be distractions that would somehow get his mind off what he'd been think-ing about since the first time he'd seen her in her fa-ther's office: being with her, knowing her, kissing her...making love to her for hours.

It was a lucky thing she didn't know how he really felt. If she had any idea that he'd been seriously at-tracted to her since before they'd ever met, she'd be even more determined. Either that, or she'd never speak to him again because she'd know who he was—and who he worked with!

Ken was mercifully saved from his musings when the car pulled off the highway onto a twisty mountain road. Every hundred feet or so, he was able to spot well-lit signs advertising their destination. The Little Love Nest seemed to have a strong affinity for the color pink. They also appeared to love hearts—judging by the shape of the signs—and nauseatingly cute little bare-ass cupids complete with arrows.

"I am having a very bad feeling about this," he mut-tered under his breath as they rounded the final bend and saw the resort in all its glory.

"Oh, boy," Pamela whispered when she saw it too.

The building was impressive. Sprawling, three sto-ries, with columns, balconies and balustrades lining the front facade. It stood at the foot of a steep hillside, fac-ing the lake. Ken imagined that in the light of day the vista would be tremendous.

"Nice view," Pamela offered weakly.

Yeah. Nice view. Which was required when the building itself was painted a hideously awful shade of pink that hurt the eyes. It was like someone had poured a mountain of melted raspberry sherbet over the stucco, then trimmed it with dark red strips of licorice. "All we need are Hansel and Gretel to tell us if the witch is home," Ken muttered.

The floodlights on the front lawn illuminated small groups of topiaries, cut into heart and cupid shapes. Ken thought he saw a swan dozing near a small pond, which was framed by three vine-covered gazebos. A romantic swing, the perfect size for two, hung from a towering tree. They passed a small wishing well and Ken was able to make out a sign on it, which read, Wishes Cost A Kiss. Wishes That Come True Cost A Thousand Kisses.

He rolled his eyes and grimaced. The whole place was so cheesily romantic he found himself wishing he'd grabbed an airsick bag from the plane!

A woman stood at the bottom of the front steps, obviously waiting to greet them. As the car pulled to a stop, she opened Ken's door. "Welcome to The Little Love Nest. We're so pleased you've decided to share the most special vacation you'll ever enjoy right here with us."

Ken stepped out of the car, getting a good look at the woman under the lights, and watched Pamela to gauge her reaction as she did the same. Probably in her early sixties, their hostess wore a white spandex jumpsuit, trimmed with pink rosebuds at each cuff and around the neck. High spike-heeled shoes gave her a few extra inches of height. Somehow, in spite of her age, she managed to carry off the ensemble. "I'm Miss Mona, the owner of this establishment," she said, her voice a husky purr, "and I am here to make certain you have the most sensual and deliciously erotic time of your lives."

Sensual? Deliciously erotic? Oh, hell!

"Believe me, I'm an expert in male-female relationships, having been in the field all my life. And what I've created here is the perfect atmosphere for newly married couples to kick off their lives together with a veritable explosion of delight."

"In the field? Are you a marriage counselor?" Pamela asked.

The woman gave a light laugh. "Oh, no, no, my experience has been much more *hands-on*, you could say. I've owned establishments like this in the past, but they were for couples who were, uh, less *committed* to each other than my clientele here."

Ken suddenly understood what she was talking about. Pamela still looked confused. He hoped she didn't ask any more questions. In case his suspicions were correct, he didn't really think he wanted Miss Mona talking about her days in the bordello business.

"Al will bring your bags, let me show you to your rooms. Tomorrow is soon enough for the full tour."

They fell into step behind Miss Mona, Pamela looking around wide-eyed as they entered the hotel. The place was quiet, eerily so. Ken didn't even spot anyone working behind the check-in desk.

"More swans," Ken muttered, noticing two of the birds reclining near a huge fountain that dominated the center of the courtyard-type lobby. Faux Grecian statues of well-endowed naked men and buxom women lined the fountain, spilling water from plaster urns...not to mention bodily orifices. Ken just shook his head. Then he saw the statuary lining the hallway past the fountain.

"Oh, my goodness," he heard Pamela whisper as she paused to stare goggle-eyed at a statue depicting a naked couple making love. The pose was a little too familiar—with the man's mouth on the woman's breast, and her head thrown back in ecstasy as she kept her legs tightly wrapped around him. "They're..."

If she said it, he thought he just might have to punch a hole in the wall. Grabbing her arm, he tugged her along, nearly causing her to stumble, but not caring. The very last thing he needed was for Miss-I-Need-It-Now to get any more ideas!

His own steps slowed when he saw the next statue standing in a discreet alcove set into the wall of the corridor. This one showed a couple engaged in *oral* activities. *Simultaneous* oral activities.

There was no dragging Pamela past it.

"Oh, my gosh, are they doing what I think they're doing?"

"Can we please go to our room?" Ken bit out between tightly clenched teeth, wondering how she managed to make him even hotter with this innocent act than she had on the plane with her blatant suggestiveness.

"How can her back arch that far?"

"It's a statue, Pamela."

"But is it possible?"

Miss Mona paused in front of them, watching over her shoulder in amusement.

"Pamela, please," Ken muttered.

"I mean, that looks painful!"

"Oh, my dear, this *is* going to be a special honeymoon," the hostess said. "And don't worry, you're tall."

Pamela gave her a puzzled expression. "Tall?"

Miss Mona gave her a nod and a mysterious smile. She met Ken's eye, raising one brow as if to ask if he knew what she was talking about. Hell, yes, he knew what she was talking about! As soon as Pamela had stopped to gawk at the statue he'd had a mental image of just how perfectly matched their bodies were for certain intimacies.

Ken mumbled a curse word under his breath. When he finally managed to get Pamela moving again, he sent up a silent prayer that there would be no more statuary between them and their room. No such luck. But at least she didn't start asking too many questions about the next one. She gave it one shocked stare, obviously recognizing what the couple—both on all fours—were doing, and walked on.

Miss Mona finally stopped a few feet before they reached another statue alcove, leading Ken to think that maybe his luck was changing. He didn't know if he could handle another blatantly sexual exhibition, nor Pamela's reaction to it!

"Are you ready?" Miss Mona asked, pausing dramatically with one hand on the doorknob. Ken nearly had a heart attack on the spot when he noticed their room number. *Sixty-nine? Could things get any worse?*

"I am *so* ready," Pamela said, her voice shaking.

Yeah, Ken was *so* ready too. So ready to get the hell out of here and hightail it back to Miami before all his good intentions fled and he showed Pamela what Miss Mona had meant about her being "tall." *Yes, they'd fit together very well.* She damn sure wouldn't have to arch her back too far if they got a little oral.

Thrusting that numbingly erotic mental image out of his brain, he watched as their hostess opened the door to their room.

"Ah, ah," Miss Mona said as Pamela moved past him. "Haven't you forgotten something?" They both stared. "Isn't it customary for the groom to carry the bride across the threshold?"

The woman obviously wasn't going to take no for an answer. Gritting his teeth, Ken grabbed Pamela and picked her up, ignoring her start of surprise. For such a tall woman, she didn't weigh much. He willed himself not to notice how perfectly she fit in his arms.

"Much better," Mona said with a nod.

The woman reached around the door to flip on the light. Ken paused to force a surreal sense of calm to descend as he prepared for whatever he was going to find in their suite. Then he stepped inside. It was a good thing he'd paused to prepare himself. "It's a bordello," he muttered, standing just inside the door with Pamela still in his arms.

The pink cupids and hearts were gone. All the sickeningly sweet romantic trappings had faded away just past the lobby. Here, in this room, the atmosphere screamed one thing: raw, sexual need. He could only wonder what Miss Mona was thinking as she watched the two of them staring around the place, their eyes wide, their mouths hanging open.

"I'll leave you two alone," she said with a pleased,

knowing smile. Before she left, Al arrived with their luggage, placed it inside the room, and followed Miss Mona out without saying a word.

The click of the door echoed loudly in the silence, reminding Ken of the firing of a starter's pistol. *Let the games begin!* After all, that's what this room was entirely about.

Games. Adult games. Erotic, sexual games.

From the rich burgundy carpeting to the heavy golden drapes on the windows, the suite was bathed in deep sensuous color. Lying before a huge double-sided fireplace, a thick, white rug provided a splash of brightness. It was, of course, the perfect size for two. He couldn't stop a mental picture of Pamela's thick dark hair against that white rug, knowing how much she'd enjoy the sensuality of her naked skin against the soft faux fur. Shaking off the image, he continued to look around.

Next to the rug rose a circular staircase. Ken slowly allowed his gaze to travel up it. The steps wound around a tall champagne-glass shaped bathtub.

Bubbles and firelight. Mood music and rich colors. Erotic paintings on the walls.

Yes, things had definitely gotten worse.

Then he spied the chaise lounge, complete with velvet ropes discreetly draped across the curved headrest, and visualized the possibilities of *that* particular piece of furniture.

Mental images of cold showers and wrinkled old people getting it on were not stopping his body's reaction. He kept holding Pamela in his arms, knowing if he let her down she'd be *sure* to notice his physical response.

Besides, she was too busy taking in every inch of the room, with her mouth hanging open, to demand that he release her.

"Guess I'm going to get to look at that after all," she said softly. He followed her gaze. A huge hardcover edition of the *Kama Sutra* stood prominently on one of the side tables, right next to a room service menu, which was opened to a page displaying the various sex toys for sale in the gift shop.

They both continued to look around, their eyes falling almost in unison on the sensuously draped bed. The sensuously draped *round* bed. Right below the mirrored ceiling.

Pamela finally looked up at him, her face flushed. "Wow."

Ken muttered, "Welcome to the best little whorehouse in Tahoe."

A seductive smile curled across her lips. "Ken, remember that platonic honeymoon idea?" Her arms tightened around his neck and she pressed closer until he could feel the jut of her pointed nipples against his chest.

He nodded warily. "I remember."

"Sorry to tell you this, darling. But you are *totally* screwed."

7

AFTER HER audacious proclamation, Ken dropped her to her feet. Grabbing his suitcase, he marched across the room and tossed it in a corner. "I'm taking a shower," he growled as he grabbed some clean clothes.

"Want me to scrub your back?" she offered, laughing throatily as he glared at her from across the dimly lit suite.

Once he was gone, Pamela began exploring the room in earnest. There was no question that this was a rather *unusual* honeymoon resort.

There was no television, though she noticed a sign saying that TV's and VCR's could be requested, along with a complete stock of erotic movies. "No, thanks," she said aloud, dropping the card back onto the table.

The brochure of special amenities offered by the hotel was certainly interesting. Massages. Herbal wraps. Naked Jell-O Twister in a rubber-floored room. "Might have to try that one."

Mirrors graced every wall. Heady, musky incense was provided on a bedside table. Outside was a very private covered patio, with screens laced with fragrant vines that made it seem like a completely secluded forest grove. A two-person spa stood in one corner. It looked warm and inviting, particularly in the cool night air. A sign beside it read Due To The Delicate Balance Of Moisturizing Oils, No Clothing Of Any Type Is Allowed In The Spa.

"Convenient," she said with a grin, hoping she was going to be soothing some aching muscles in that hot water before too many days had passed. She hoped she had some *unusual* aches—from muscles that hadn't been given a very vigorous workout thus far in her virginal life.

The bed fascinated her. She'd never in her life seen a round bed, didn't even know such things were made. But somehow Madame Mona—she imagined the title madame suited her—had found one. When she pulled back the crushed velvet burgundy bedspread, trying to figure out how on earth one would find bedding to fit, she immediately noticed the black satin sheets. "Slippery," she mused, her mind filling with delicious images of rolling around on the bed. Naked. And definitely *not* alone.

Okay, Pamela, you got him here. Now it's time to put your money where your mouth is. And your body where your mouth wants to be!

Knowing she couldn't count on Ken remaining in the shower much longer, she grabbed her suitcase and dug through it until she found the nightie she was looking for. Black leather wouldn't be quite as dramatic next to the black sheets, though she imagined it would be quite interesting another night, perhaps against the backdrop of the thick white rug in front of the fireplace. Tonight, however, white would do the trick.

By the time she heard the shower turn off, she'd

brushed her hair, touched up her makeup, donned the so-sheer-it-was-nearly-invisible nightgown, and somehow managed not to throw up in terror.

She wouldn't have to *do* anything, would she? He was a guy. He was dying for her—she knew that much. Just seeing her like this, would he need any further incentive to forget his silly ideas of a platonic relationship? She hoped she wouldn't have to talk him into it, for heaven's sake. Frankly, Pamela didn't know if her ego could take it.

No, they couldn't talk about it. Either he would see her, want her, act on it, or she was going to throw her hands up in surrender and go to sleep.

She waited, standing beside the bed, hardly breathing as she wondered which it was going to be.

KEN SHOWERED for as long as possible, leaning against the white and black tiles and letting an ice-cold stream of water subdue the raging hormones he'd been dealing with for hours.

"Let her be asleep," he muttered under his breath. "She has *got* to be asleep."

Finally, when he knew he was on the verge of hypothermia, he got out, toweled off and grabbed the clean sweatpants he'd brought in from his suitcase. Hopefully, Pamela would be dressed in a similar fashion! After all, she barely knew him. She was probably suddenly feeling very uncertain and uncomfortable, and would back off the seduction routine now that he was in a position to call her bluff. At least, so he hoped. So he prayed.

When he walked out of the frigid bathroom into the suite, and saw her standing beside the bed, bathed in the golden glow of a dozen candles she'd lit around the room, he knew heaven had not heard his prayers.

The nightgown didn't cover her, it merely floated around her. Wispy. Sheer. Seductive and inviting. As sinful as only the color white could be when draping the form of a beautiful woman.

The tiny spaghetti straps barely held the top up over her breasts, and he saw her dark, tight nipples only a centimeter below the fabric's edge. Remembering the taste of her, his breathing slowed, his heartbeat increased.

The silky material gathered tightly at her waist, then fell in sleek undulating folds to the floor. But there were no sides. At the sight of her bare hip, her long, slim legs, the dark patch of hair at the top of her thighs, Ken almost gave in. He almost reached for her, almost pulled her to the bed. He almost buried himself so deep inside her body that he didn't know if he'd ever find his way out again.

Sanity intruded. "You. Get that off." He pointed toward the gown.

A slow, knowing smile curled across her lips. "My, my, so much for foreplay," she murmured as she reached to tug one minuscule strap off a shoulder.

"No! I mean, put something else on!"

"Oh, I intend to. There's something I very much want on me."

"Clothes," he managed to hiss. "I meant other clothes."

"So you prefer the black leather after all?"

"Only if it's a belt so I can spank you with it," he muttered under his breath.

Her head cocked back and her eyes widened in innocent misunderstanding. "Now who's the kinky one?"

"Pamela..."

She leaned forward, dropping to the bed on hands and knees. He had to close his eyes as she began to crawl toward him, the gown gapping away from her breasts and her hips. He remembered the last statue in the hall. Knew she remembered, too.

"You've got to be exhausted," he said hoarsely. *Get that look off your face—I am not going to do this!*

"You, too. So come to bed," she purred.

"Come on, Pamela," he finally managed to say, trying hard to sound reasonable and not on the verge of carnal meltdown. "You're overwhelmed, emotionally, physically. Go to sleep, okay? Take a big, huge T-shirt out of my suitcase, change into it and just go to sleep."

Please. Please just go to sleep before I climb on there with you, grab your hips and drive you into the headboard!

Did she see him shaking? Did she notice that the elastic waistband was no longer needed to hold his sweatpants up? There was no way in the universe they'd be able to fall down, considering that the record-setting hard-on he'd finally managed to subdue in the frigid shower was back with a vengeance.

"You don't want me?" It wasn't a question. It was a verbal challenge. She'd crossed the width of the strangely shaped bed and reached his side. Rising to her knees, she managed to slide her silk-covered form against every inch of his bare skin, from waist to shoulder, as sinuous and sensual as a cat. "You're *sure* you don't want to do this?"

What are you freakin' insane?! Hell yes...do it! a mental voice screamed.

Then her hands moved across his skin, cool, fleeting, building the fire. "I've been wanting to touch you since the minute we met," she said with a sigh. She dropped her head back, closed her eyes, smiling as she continued to drive him mad with her smooth, pale hands.

She moved her touch lower, sliding the back of her fingers down across the front of his pants, letting out a groan of pleasure at finding him so hard for her. That needy sigh, accompanied by a shudder that ran through her long, curvy body, brought him to the brink—and very nearly over it.

"Let me," she whispered, sliding her hand into the waistband of his sweatpants and moving her body lower to nibble on his chest, his stomach. Then she scraped her teeth along the edge of his sweatpants, making him shake.

Then she was *there*—breathing hotly through the fabric, cupping him with her hands as she teased him with her mouth, much as he'd done to her in the car.

"Let me give you some of what you gave me," she said with a throaty purr as she began pushing the waistband down, her sweet, wet lips curved into a sultry smile that promised pleasure beyond description.

He would have. He was that gone, that powerless as he looked down at her, watching her dark hair against his stomach, needing her—her kiss, her touch, oh, damn, her mouth!

Then came the knock. And reality.

"Room service."

Pamela had never wanted to let out such a scream of frustration as the one she choked on when Ken pulled away from her and turned toward the door. "No!"

He groaned. "No is right."

Then he walked away. At least his legs were shaky— she saw him grab the back of the chaise lounge to steady himself as he passed on his way to answer the door. She threw herself down on the bed, lying on her stomach, shaking her head back and forth. So close! She'd been so close—and so had he!

Hearing mumbled voices, she listened as Ken thanked someone, then watched as he turned around carrying a bottle of champagne and two glasses. She saw the uncomfortable look on his face and knew what he was thinking. If he offered her a drink instead of the sex she was dying for, she might just have to crack the bottle over his head.

"Champagne. Compliments of Miss Mona," he said, still standing across the room by the door. "Good timing."

She snorted in disgust. Reality, in the guise of what appeared to be a bottle of Dom Perignon, had shaken him from his sensual lethargy.

"Why don't you leave it right there?" she asked, rising to her knees on the bed, knowing it was useless but not quite willing to give up yet.

He couldn't have missed the heady invitation in her eyes.

"Uh, actually, I think I'm going to take a shower."

"You already *took* one!"

"I think I need another one." He bit each word out from between clenched teeth.

"You are a coward, Ken McBain!" she called as he walked toward the bathroom. "And since you just took a half-hour shower, I hope you run out of hot water!"

He paused, his hand on the doorknob, and looked over his shoulder. "What on earth makes you think I used any hot water the *first* time?"

When he entered the bathroom, he slammed the door behind him with such force that a painting—depicting a couple in a position Pamela doubted was humanly possible—fell right off the wall.

Rolling over, she punched the mattress, cursed the champagne bearer and wished to heaven she'd gotten to the shower first. She could definitely use some strong jets right about now!

"That's it, Ken McBain. You have lost out. The Pamela express has passed you by and is heading on down the tracks," she muttered as she yanked off the stupid white negligee and went over to dig her own T-shirt out of her suitcase. She didn't want anything of his touching her body.

Well, that was a big, fat lie. She wanted every inch of *him* touching her body. Forsaking that—as he obviously had—she wasn't in the mood for any T-shirt substitute!

As she changed, kicking the sexy nightgown under the bed in disgust, she grew more and more angry.

What was with her lately? Dammit, she was no doormat. Peter didn't want her as much as he'd wanted her father's money? Well, to heck with him. Ken wanted her but wouldn't take her? Well, to heck with him, too!

She wasn't going to beg. She wasn't going to try any more seductions that left her shaking and empty and so horny she wanted to pull her own hair out.

And she was going to tell him so—right now. Then she was going to demand that he get out of the bathroom so she could take her own shower! Or else go out on the patio and see if that damn whirlpool had seat jets!

Marching across the room, she pushed the bathroom door open and stepped inside, her eyes immediately going toward the double-size shower. It was huge, obviously built for two, with shower heads at head and waist level, plus a sturdy-looking bench seat that extended from one side to the other near the back wall. That made her angrier.

Reaching for the handle, she yanked open the misty glass door. "You just lost your best chance, mister. I'm through. Finished. Don't ever expect me to try to seduce you again."

He stood frozen, staring at her, his face a picture of sexual torment. Pamela's tirade ended as her breath exited her lungs and her last thought flew from her mind.

"Oh, my," she whispered, unable to look away.

His body was perfect. She had already seen his beautiful bare torso, complete with a light matting of black chest hair into which she'd wanted to bury her fingers. Earlier she'd longed to have a chance to nibble his thick arms, and press more hot kisses against that flat stomach so rippled with muscles.

Now she saw the rest of him—the lean hips, the long, powerful legs, and, oh, the *rest* of him.

He was fully aroused. Thick, heavy, hard. Pamela's legs went weak thinking of him, of that part of him, inside her.

Would he really fit? "Ken..."

"Ever learn how to knock?" he asked, his voice a low, husky drawl. She began shivering, from the air moistened by the cold jetting water, from the liquid desire pooling between her legs with hot, wet insistence.

She finally raised her eyes to his. "I am through playing games," she said, hearing a slight quiver in her own voice. "I know what I want. I know *who* I want."

He listened but said nothing.

"I want *you*. Ken McBain. The man who found me on the beach. The man who offered me his coat. The man who took my gown away so I wouldn't burn it. The man who showed up on that plane so he could be certain I didn't get myself hurt anymore." Her voice quivered and softened. "The man whose whispers go from my ears right through my body and make me *crazy*."

"Pam..."

"Shh," she said, holding up a hand, palm out. "I'm not a little girl. I'm not someone you need to protect. I'm someone who's about to walk out of your life because I truly can't handle this game you're playing."

"Game?" he asked, his voice low, his eyes narrowing.

She nodded. "You want me so bad you can barely walk. But instead, you'll...how did you say it? *Ease the pain* all alone. Well, maybe I need someone to help me ease my pain," she gave a bitter laugh, knowing no shower jets were ever going to make her feel what Ken could with just a whisper.

"I want that someone to be *you*. No one else. For no other reason than that for the first time in my life I know what it's like to be out of my mind wanting a man's hands on me. *Your* hands. *Your* lips. Every part of *you*, Ken. But I can't stand any more of this back and forth. Your nobility is killing me."

He wasn't looking terribly noble now. Actually he was looking terribly magnificent. She crossed her arms, holding them tightly against her body as another shiver of need coursed through her. "So take me. Or leave me. But don't expect me to ask you again."

Ken braced one hand on the tile wall and reached the other toward the spigot to turn the temperature from cold to hot. The last of his resistance dissipated under the warmth of the jetting water and the sweet need in her voice.

Leave her? He didn't think he was *ever* going to be able to leave her.

He'd been able to resist her on the plane and in the car. Been able to somehow walk away in spite of how she'd looked in her white nightgown.

But he could not hold back against the look in her eyes now. Simple, dignified honesty and heady desire combined to cast away all his doubt.

"Grab one of those, would you?" he said, nodding toward a basketful of condoms on the bathroom counter. She didn't appear any more surprised to see them in this place than he had been. Her eyes widened in understanding as she did what he asked.

Slipping one hand across her hip, he pulled her into the shower with him, bringing her tightly into his arms. Catching her mouth in a kiss that held up every bit of pent-up longing he'd ever felt for her, he was barely cognizant of her moan of pleasure. He only knew he had to have her. Had to be in her. Now. For as long as he could keep her. For as long as it lasted.

"Please, Ken," she said on a moan as she tugged her T-shirt off over her head and tossed it to the shower floor. Then she stood before him, dripping, wearing only a tiny pair of white nylon underwear that did nothing to hide the dark curls he'd been wanting to touch since he'd seen her in that nightgown. "Please don't make me wait anymore," she said softly, so softly, her voice floating over him like a caress.

He couldn't wait if his life depended on it. Taking a single pleasureful moment to move his mouth to her breast, he sucked one warm nipple between his lips. Then he pushed the tiny nylon underwear off her hips and down to the floor. Encircling her waist with his hands, he pushed her against the tiled shower wall.

"Yes," she said with a drawn-out sigh. One slim thigh rose along the outside of his legs as she leaned back, her jutting breasts irresistible. He bent for another taste, stroking her fullness, lifting it in his hand, sucking and giving her tiny love bites until she started to shake with need.

He wanted to do everything with her.

But not now. Now he just needed to be inside her.

They'd had over twenty-four hours of foreplay and if he didn't feel her wrapped around him soon, he knew he was going to erupt all over the floor of the shower like some teenage kid.

Just because he was ready, though, didn't mean for certain that she was. He had to touch her, had to make sure. Slipping his hand down her back, he caressed her hip. He felt her shudder in reaction as she lifted her leg higher. Her parted thighs invited him on and she pressed back against his hand, taunting him with the slickness of her skin, the curve of her buttocks.

Bending to kiss the hot skin at her nape, he pulled her closer, higher. Then he slipped his finger between the backs of her taut thighs, liking how she hissed, loving how she rocked against his hand and pleaded, low and incoherent.

Her flesh was swollen, wet, and his fingers sunk into her easily, causing them both to moan.

"I need...please, Ken, now!" she ordered.

He didn't need any further encouragement, pausing only to tear open one of the condom packets and sheathe himself. She reached to help, but he grabbed both of her hands in one of his and lifted them high above her head, knowing if she touched him he might just lose his mind.

She squirmed against the wall, arching her back, thrusting her breasts toward him and he couldn't resist. He kissed one perfect dark nipple, then the other, and she shuddered and whimpered, twisting her body beneath his mouth.

"Now, please, Ken. Please take me now," she urged.

She hooked her leg behind his knee, tilted farther, rubbed herself against him. She was wet everywhere. Hot, wet, completely ready. And he simply couldn't wait.

Releasing her hands, he picked her up. He wrapped both of her thighs around his hips, pressed her back into the wall, and pulled her closer, nudging her dark curls apart with his erection. Catching her mouth with his in another breath-stealing kiss, he pushed into her.

She hissed when he entered her, but kept her arms wrapped in a death grip around his shoulders.

"Tight," he muttered, not believing how good she felt, how wet, warm, and unbelievably *tight*. He wanted to go slow for her, wanted to slide into her inch by inch, but his body was urging him to plunge in, make her his, make her scream and then make her come over and over again.

Pamela must have sensed his restraint. She pushed against him, tightened her legs, grabbed his hair with both hands and caught his mouth in a hot, carnal kiss. "Now," she ordered against his lips as she pressed frantic kisses against his face. "Now."

He couldn't wait. Ken drove home with a hard thrust and brought their bodies as close together as it was possible for two adults to be. He was so deep inside her he could feel her flesh spasming against him as shudders wracked through her body. He didn't move at first, just savored the wet heat, wondered if he'd ever experienced anything even close to the physical pleasure engulfing him now—and knew he hadn't.

"Yes," Pamela whispered, kissing the side of his neck

and keeping her face buried there. She clung to him, feeling tears in her eyes as she acknowledged that it had finally happened. He was inside her, completely inside her body.

There were no fireworks, no instant orgasmic explosions. In fact it was awkward. She felt stretched, a little uncomfortable. But she also felt so close to him. Cherished. And so deliciously filled. She didn't want him to stop, didn't want it to end.

He drew back from her, and Pamela pulled his face closer, keeping her own buried against his neck, not wanting him to see her tears. He kissed her neck, slid his tongue along her collarbone, gave one tantalizing nip to her shoulder. The water continued to pound on them, warm and steady, and slowly Pamela felt her body relax, her skin stretch and accept.

His kisses helped. He moved lower, tasting, sipping of her, starting those crazy sweet love bites on her breast. The pain continued to fade and she felt herself growing more restless. Wanting more. Wanting what was next.

As if sensing her anxiousness, Ken slowly pulled back, then slid into her again. She sucked in a breath, a little scared, a lot excited. She wiggled her behind against his hands, saw how her every movement affected him. Tentatively squeezing him deep inside, she loved how his eyes flew open and a groan escaped his lips.

He stared down at her, a ragged smile on his handsome face. "You keep doing that and I can't guarantee this is going to last much longer."

She smiled and did it again.

"Witch," he muttered.

Stepping toward the back of the shower, Ken lowered one of her legs until her foot rested on the bench seat. She'd wondered, when she first saw it, why it was connected only to the sides of the shower, not to the back. Now, seeing the possibilities, she thought she understood. It would be very easy to sit with her legs on either side. A thrill of excitement went through her as she thought of straddling him, being in control.

He slowly drew almost all the way out of her, and Pamela leaned back, keeping her eyes closed as the water continued to pelt them. Then he stopped. Didn't move. Didn't plunge into her as she'd expected.

Opening her eyes, she saw Ken staring down at her upraised thigh. His eyes were narrowed, and he slowly shook his head. As he lifted his gaze to her face, she saw his confusion and realized he'd seen flecks of red on her skin.

"Tell me this wasn't your first time."

She said nothing.

After a few seconds, when he saw she wasn't going to deny it, he pulled his body completely out of hers, let go of the one leg he still held around his hips, and stepped back. "You're a virgin?"

"Not anymore," she whispered.

He groaned. "Why didn't you tell me?"

"Does it matter?"

"Yes, it matters. Hell, Pamela, I sure would have gone about this a different way if I knew you'd never done it before!"

She raised a challenging brow. "Gone about this a different way? Like no way at all?"

"So you didn't tell me because you knew I wouldn't make love to you if I knew you were a virgin?" She remained silent, daring him to tell the truth. Finally, he ran a hand over his brow and said, "You're probably right." He gave a heavy sigh and leaned on the opposite wall of the shower. "Damn."

"Don't. Please, don't feel whatever it is you're feeling. Don't say anything to try to explain it away or pacify me. I wanted this. I wanted this with you. Now. Tonight."

Staring at her, he reached out to brush some wet strands of hair away from her brow. With one thumb, he wiped moisture away from the corner of her eye and smiled at her tenderly. "I know. I'm sorry, sweetheart. I'm so sorry I hurt you."

She bit her lip, feeling tears rise again at his tenderness, wondering how on earth a man so big, so handsome and strong, could know exactly what to say to leave her weak-kneed and quivering. "I'm all right."

Reaching for a washcloth that hung on a rack behind them, he soaked it, then gently pushed her toward the bench. "Let me take care of you," he whispered.

Pamela let him lower her to the bench, twisting her body so her back rested against the shower wall. He lifted one of her thighs, parting her, exposing her. Pamela watched, feeling the excitement rise again as he knelt on the floor of the shower in front of her.

"So sorry," he whispered as he took the cloth and gently, tenderly, washed away the small amount of blood from her skin. Then the cloth was gone, there was no barrier between the warmth of his hand and her own achingly tender flesh.

A moan escaped her lips as he touched her. He slid his fingers through the slick folds of her body and expertly stroked her right where she needed his touch most. "Yes," she whispered, closing her eyes as she gave in to sensation.

He built the heat again, not merely with his hands, but with his mouth. Ken pressed kiss after kiss on her arms, her neck, her lips. Then he moved lower, paying lavish attention to her breasts, sucking a nipple deep into his mouth just as he slid one finger deep into her body.

She jerked up, thrust against his hand, restless and wanting more. He knew. Kept stroking, kept kissing. Moved lower. And then his mouth was there, sweetly tasting her.

"Oh, please," she muttered hoarsely when she felt his tongue slide into her.

He didn't stop. Drawing her thighs farther apart, he used his mouth and his hands to bring her to the edge, bring her to a quivering mass of sensation.

But it wasn't quite enough.

"I need you inside me when you make this happen again," she whispered, her voice thick and demanding. "Please, don't make me fall alone this time."

He didn't hesitate. As he rose to stand next to her, Pamela saw that he was still as thick and erect as before, and her mouth went dry. She wanted him inside her when he made her explode.

She pulled him down so he sat facing her, both of them straddling the bench. Instinct told her what to do and his eyes darkened as she moved over him.

"Take your time, sweetheart," he whispered as he cupped her face. "You are in control here."

That thought thrilled her. In control. Of this luscious, caring man. For a few minutes, anyway, he was giving her the power to do what she wanted, take what she needed.

She needed everything.

Moving closer, she slid her thighs over his and pushed him into a reclining position on the bench. Then she slid up his wet body, kissing his chest, nibbling on his neck and finally catching his mouth with her own. "I'm in control," she whispered against his lips.

Then she lowered herself onto his erection, noting how smooth it was, how his caresses had made her so wet he slid into her with ease.

He groaned as she engulfed him. Pamela closed her eyes, taking him deeper until he was fully inside her. She remained still, noting that there was no pain this time. Still the fullness, but now only pleasure. Then she began to move, to ride him, sighing with every stroke.

Ken held her hips and moved below her, matching her pace. Their movements grew more frenzied until Pamela began to gasp with the intensity of it all. Then Ken moved his hands to her stomach. And lower.

He parted her curls with his fingers, and began to stroke her, matching each sweet flick of his finger to each strong thrust inside her. He brought her to the precipice again until she was shuddering with the pleasure of it.

And this time, when he brought her to that shattering convulsion of pure physical energy, he fell right along with her.

AT SOME POINT, after their bodies had become pruney, Ken turned off the shower and carried Pamela out of it. He toweled her off with one of the thick, fluffy bath sheets, then wrapped her in it while he dried himself.

She didn't even try to speak. A languorous smile curled across those gorgeous lips and her eyes were heavy—tired, but filled with pleasure. He liked that he put that look on her face. Correction, he *loved* that he put that look on her face.

Her every movement was lethargic, boneless and sated. When he picked her up to carry her into the bedroom, she curled against him as if they were two halves of a whole.

Tomorrow reality would intrude. Somehow he'd have to deal with the guilt that was already wracking his brain. He'd made love to her, a beautiful, needy virgin he hardly knew. A woman who'd been set to marry someone else. A woman who didn't even know why he was really here with her.

There was no changing what had already happened, however, and plenty of time to worry about it later. So, for tonight, he simply allowed himself the pleasure of holding her sweet, sleeping body in his arms.

8

KEN WOKE UP the next morning certain the person who'd invented the round bed was a sadist. Probably worked for the Spanish Inquisition in another life.

"Pure torture," he mumbled, knowing he'd never had a more restless night.

There was no way to sleep apart on the round monstrosity. If he moved away from Pamela toward his side of the bed, either his feet fell off at one end, or his head the other. The insidious thing was designed to keep two people firmly in the middle, spooning, or wrapped around one another, all night long. Which was probably fine and dandy for most people staying in this room.

But not for him.

"Damn," he whispered as streaks of light began to sift in from the heavily draped windows. Though it was barely seven, there was no sense remaining in bed. He wouldn't be able to go back to sleep. Nothing *else* was going to happen either.

During the night, when he'd rolled over several times to find Pamela's naked body curled up against every inch of his own, he'd been sorely tempted to kiss her awake. He wanted to show her what languorous late-night lovemaking could be like. Wanted to take his time, caress and stroke every inch of her, to make up for what had happened earlier.

Her first time *ever* making love and he'd shoved her up against the wall of a shower. *Stupid, McBain!* Exciting, yes. Amazingly fulfilling, too. Still stupid, though.

She deserved more. So much more. And he was dying to give it to her. But he wouldn't.

Ken gently moved her arm from across his chest and slid out from under the silky black sheets, wondering how many people had rolled over and fallen onto the floor in this place. Behind him, Pamela sighed and snuggled deeper under the covers, probably missing his body heat. He had to force himself to turn away and pull on some clothes. Then he escaped to the patio.

Though the middle of summer, compared to Miami, where he'd been living for the past month, the morning mountain air was downright chilly. The climate was even cooler than at home in northern Virginia. He thought about going back inside but needed to be alone, to think about what to do next.

Go back to bed.

No, that was out. He couldn't get close to her again, as much as he wanted to.

There was no longer any question of staying away from her in order to protect his own emotions. Yes, he'd used his failed relationship with Liz as a mental barrier, sticking by his mantra of "no women on the rebound" even when he knew Pamela was nothing like his ex. Somehow, however, that concern no longer applied. Frankly, having spent hours talking to her yesterday and the night before, he was having serious doubts about how much Pamela had cared for Peter anyway.

"Pamela and Peter." He stretched out in a lounge chair, shielded from view all around by the thick vine-covered trellis encircling the patio. "How could you even stand the sound of your names together?" he mused aloud.

No, he truly didn't believe, deep down, that Pamela was mourning the end of her engagement. Nor did he think less of her for that. He'd seen the confusion in her eyes more than once when she'd discussed Peter's whirlwind courtship, which had seemed too good to be true. She'd seemed anything but devastated. Embarrassed? Yes. Humiliated? That, too. But her heart wasn't broken. Not by a long shot.

Ken no longer felt he had to keep her at arm's length until she got over Peter. She didn't have to get over him. She'd never been *under* him, emotionally or physically.

"Thank God," he muttered, still glad to know she'd never completely given herself over to her ex.

Or to any man. Until last night. With him.

And that was exactly the problem. It had been bad enough when he feared she was a vulnerable woman on the rebound. Now he knew the truth. Okay, maybe she was emotionally accessible. But the fact that she had never been involved in a physical relationship increased the stakes a hundredfold.

Standing to peer through the thick hedge, he caught a glimpse of the morning sunlight shimmering on the surface of the lake at the bottom of the hill, and his breath caught. He wanted to share it with her. The morning. The sunrise. Many more nights like last night. Lots and lots of showers.

He'd been half gone on the woman before they'd ever met. Now...well, now he felt something like a cliff diver who'd leaped off a mountainside in Hawaii into the cool blue waters of the Pacific—over his head and sinking fast.

If he wanted any kind of chance at all of letting things develop between them, he had to be honest with her. He wasn't much better than Peter in that regard. No, he didn't work directly for her father, wasn't using her as a stepping-stone. Ken's contract with Bradford Investments to update the entire corporate software system had been signed and sealed before Ken ever knew Pamela Bradford existed.

That didn't change the fact that he worked *with* her father. That he'd seen what had happened at the hotel. That her father was the one who'd pleaded with him to go with her to Tahoe.

Once she found out the truth, she wouldn't stay around for more than the ninety seconds it would take her to slap his face. The only chance he had of making her stick around for longer was to show her how good they could be together—and not just physically. That was a given. They'd proven it last night—proven it beyond all doubt—to the point where he got the shakes even thinking about it. Being with her. Being *in* her. How her eyes darkened and her lips parted when he touched her. That sweet little sound she made in the back of her throat—a tiny helpless cry as her body shook in orgasm. *Snap out of it!*

He had to get past the physical and make her know him, trust him, so that when he told her the truth maybe it could be a beginning for them...rather than the end.

Until then, he couldn't make love to her again, though that might be the death of him. The guilt wouldn't let him. Not while he wasn't being honest with her.

That was the plan at least. But like she'd said in the car last night...lately he really sucked at sticking to his own plans.

PAMELA AWOKE to an empty bed and at first wondered if last night had been a dream. Had she and Ken really made heated love in the shower? Had he truly held her in his arms until she fell asleep? Rolling toward the other side of the bed, she caught the warm, masculine scent on the other pillow and hugged it close. *Not a dream.*

Getting out of bed, she retrieved the silky robe that matched the white nightie she'd worn briefly the night before. It did nothing to keep out the chill but was all she had. Then she went looking for Ken. "Good morning," she said when she found him sitting on the patio.

He gave her a lazy smile and held out a hand for her to join him. "Good morning yourself." He scooted over, making room for her on the lounge chair. She sat down and curled up against him, resting her arm across his chest and her head in the crook of his arm, finding warmth in his embrace.

"You okay this morning?"

She heard the real question he was asking and knew

he was still thinking about the fact that she'd been a virgin until a few hours ago. "I'm fine." Sliding one thigh over both of his, she curled closer and pressed a soft kiss against his neck. "Better than fine."

"Good," he said softly as he stroked one hand up and down her back, making her shiver. Not from cold. She was feeling very warm, verging on hot.

"So what do you want to do today, on this first official day of our honeymoon?" Ken asked.

"Stay in bed?" When he didn't respond, she asked warily, "Ken, what's wrong?" Pulling away to look up at him, she noticed a slight frown on his face. "Please don't tell me you're having regrets."

"No regrets, Pam," he assured her. "You?"

"Not on your life."

He chuckled at the obvious vehemence in her voice.

"So what's the problem? Why can't we go back inside, order pancakes with whipped cream for breakfast, then save the whipped cream for later instead?" She wagged her eyebrows suggestively.

A rueful smile crossed his lips. "Pamela, I don't regret last night. But I still don't think we should be jumping into anything here. Maybe we should slow down, take our time."

She wasn't prepared for that. "Isn't that kind of like shutting the barn door after the mare already got out and partied all night with the stallion down in the far pasture?"

"You and your horse analogies," he muttered.

"Ya big stud." He laughed and hugged her closer to

his chest, but she noticed the laughter didn't quite reach his eyes. "Why? What's holding us back?"

He took a deep breath and looked like he was about to speak. Then he sighed and glanced away.

"Ken?"

"I just don't think either one of us is ready for this," he finally said.

"Speak for yourself."

"Okay, I will," he said, his tone serious. "I spent three months last year getting involved with a woman who, it turned out, was definitely *not* over her ex. And I've sworn that I'd never put myself in that situation again."

Pamela didn't quite know what to say. Part of her ached for him, part of her wanted to slap whoever the woman was who'd dared to hurt him. Another part was relieved. *Her idiocy...my gain!*

"I'm sorry you were hurt."

He shrugged and shook his head. "Not hurt, at least not long-term. I hadn't lost my head—or my heart. And Liz ended up with the right guy, although there's no denying my pride was hurt."

"I know a little something about that one."

He squeezed her shoulders. "Mostly it was a wake-up call. It definitely made me more cautious about the women I date. No one wants to be used."

She heard his next thought, though it remained unspoken. *You of all people should understand that.*

True. She did understand that. Remembering the devastation she'd felt when she'd learned Peter had merely been using her to get ahead with her father, Pamela tilted her head down and bit her bottom lip.

Since the minute she'd met Ken on the beach she'd been selfish. First wanting him to ease the hurt of Peter's actions, then wanting Ken to help her explore all the pent-up passion buried deep inside her. She hadn't taken a moment to think about his feelings, though he'd voiced them several times.

"I've been pretty awful," she whispered.

"That's not true—"

She cut him off. "It is. You're right. I used you, Ken. You told me how you felt and I completely ignored what you wanted and thought only of myself."

She'd been as selfish as his ex—to this wonderful man who'd been nothing but good to her since the moment they'd met. It wasn't a pleasant realization.

"You're right," she murmured. "You're right, and I'm sorry."

"Don't be sorry. Hey, maybe last night had to happen. The two of us have been striking sparks off each other since the minute we met."

She couldn't contain a smile. "True."

"So maybe we needed to act on them," he continued, "to douse the fire before we sent this whole place up in flames."

"And now that we've doused the fire, is it completely out?"

He must have heard the uncertainty in her tone because he tipped her chin up with one finger and looked deeply into her eyes. "Not by a long shot, Pamela. Just banked for a little while. I know it could burn out of control in a heartbeat, if we let it."

"And you don't want to let it?" It wasn't really a question.

"Do you?"

"Do you want me to be honest, or do you want me to lie?"

He laughed out loud and shook his head. "You are a joy, Pamela Bradford, do you know that? I don't think I've ever known a woman as relentlessly honest and forthright as you."

"Okay, so being totally honest...yes, I'd love to make you burn, Ken McBain."

His eyes darkened, his jaw clenched. Beneath her fingers, she felt his heart begin to pound in his chest and knew that if she pushed him, she could change his mind.

But where would that leave her? Satisfied in the short term—very satisfied, if last night was anything to go on. Yet what about later? She sensed this man could mean much more to her than a week of all-out passion and erotic indulgence. A week was nothing. Because somehow, some way, she sensed he could mean a lifetime of happily ever afters.

Crazy, given their short-term relationship. Crazy, perhaps, but true. She knew to the depths of her heart, in a way she'd never been completely certain of with Peter, that in Ken she might have found someone with whom she could fall head over heels in love. She'd known it from the very beginning. From the moment he'd handed her his coat.

"But I also understand that we've gone a little too fast," she admitted softly, confused still by the emotional floodgate coursing through her mind. How could she be so sure? After the fiasco with Peter, she should have been questioning her own judgment, but she wasn't.

Somehow, deep down, she knew something very special was happening with her and Ken. Like all good things, that was worth waiting for. "I'm willing to take it down a notch, if you are. After all, we have a week here."

"And I'm sure there's a lot to do."

"Oh, absolutely. Horseback riding, kayaking, naked Jell-O Twister."

He choked out a laugh. "You're kidding me."

"Nope. They have an entire game menu."

"I think I missed that," he said. Almost looking afraid to ask, he said, "What kind of games?"

"I didn't go down the entire list. But it appears they have lots of role-playing games, complete with costumes."

A grin quirked his lips. "See anything interesting?"

"You could be a Texas Ranger and get those spurs you were talking about."

"I don't think I'll need them."

"No, you definitely didn't fall off," she said with a giggle.

"Ha."

"Okay, at least *I* didn't fall off. They also have lots of board games."

"Board games? Sure, we'll sit around and play Clue for six days."

She cast him a sideways glance through her lowered

lashes. "Mr. McBain did it in the shower with his very big lead pipe."

He responded by tickling her until she almost fell off the lounge chair. "No, no," she squealed, trying to wiggle away. "No fair. I'm way too ticklish!"

He relented and tugged her back down to lie across his chest. "Anyone ever tell you you've got a wicked tongue, Pamela Bradford?"

"Wouldn't you like to know?" she said, giving him a sultry, moist-lipped grin.

His eyes darkened. "Oh, yeah," he replied, the heat factor intensifying. Then he sighed. "But not today."

"Right," she agreed, pretending she wasn't disappointed.

"Anyway I should have said 'smart mouth,'" he continued. "I bet you drove your parents crazy when you were growing up."

She nodded and cuddled closer, her body seeking his warmth. "Pretty much. My mother says 'why' was the first word in my vocabulary. Quickly followed by 'no.'"

"My mother taught my sisters that 'no' should be the first word in *every* girl's vocabulary."

She grinned. "How many?"

"Three. All younger."

"Bet they loved having your friends around."

"It took almost a whole year for me to figure out why all my buddies on the football team always wanted to hang out at my house after practice, and never anyone else's."

She curled her fingers around his neck and gave a wistful sigh. "Sounds wonderful."

"How about you?"

"Only child. Which I always regretted. I guess that's why I like working with kids now."

"You talked about your job on the plane," he said, smoothing back a lock of hair from her brow. "You work with troubled teens, right?"

She nodded. "At a recreation and counseling center in downtown Miami. That smart mouth comes in handy sometimes. It's hard to know the right thing to say to even your normal, all-American teenager. Trying to help the kinds of kids I meet on a daily basis, I have to be able to talk on their level, to give as good as I get, to make sure they know I'm not going to put up with any of their bull. Then, slowly, they'll start to open up to me."

He tucked her hair behind her ear and pressed a soft kiss on the top of her head. "I'm sure they're crazy about you."

"Not usually," she said with a rueful grin. "Not at first, anyway. It generally takes a while to break through. I always try to find some common ground. Being able to kick some butt on the basketball court helps. I sometimes play the kids for talking points."

He shook his head. "Not following."

"We'll play one-on-one," she explained. "For every shot I get on them, they've got to open up, to talk, to listen. It's a way of maintaining a dialogue with some teenagers who would otherwise never dream of interacting with an adult."

"Smart idea."

"You've got to use what you've got. My friend La-

Vyrle gets the girls to talk to her by doing their nails. The longer the acrylic, the longer the conversation."

"Sounds like you're a good team."

They lay in the lounge chair as the sun rose higher, casting warmth inside the shadowed, sheltered patio. Pamela didn't know when the last time was that she'd spent so much time just talking to a man. Certainly she'd talked to Peter. But now, when she looked back on it, she acknowledged that he'd merely done a lot of nodding and agreeing with whatever she said. Ken didn't. He baited her, teased her, challenged her. They got into a ten-minute debate on whether or not Michael Jordan could stage yet another comeback—which she was firmly convinced could happen.

He opened up, too. Making her smile when he reminisced about his sisters, making her frown when he told her about his ex-girlfriend. He discussed his company and, for the first time, she realized how successful a man he was. He and the half-dozen software engineers he employed worked on the kind of contracts that had to be raking in some big bucks. Very big. And yet he'd still walked away from it to come on a spur-of-the-moment trip with her. To protect her. To get to know her.

To make her fall in love with him.

Well, maybe that hadn't been what he'd set out to do. But she had a feeling it might be the end result.

She found warmth, solace and strength in his arms. She loved his laugh, loved the way his silver eyes sparkled in the sunlight. Their laughter eventually led to kisses and slow, tender caresses. Nothing more, even though she knew they both wanted more.

Finally, as if knowing if they remained wrapped around each other exchanging warm, lazy, open-mouthed kisses, they'd go further than either of them meant to, he moved away from her. "You hungry? It's almost lunchtime."

"Starved," she said. "I hope they serve more than oysters and champagne in this place."

He nodded. "Food. And if it's all oysters and champagne, we'll find the game room and go for some of that Jell-O."

THE RESORT, as it turned out, had a fantastic restaurant. In keeping with the rest of The Little Love Nest, the tables in the small, intimate café were secluded, screened with palms and white trellises. The décor wasn't nearly as garish as in other parts of the hotel, and the food was to die for. Pamela ate like she hadn't eaten in days, leaning over to steal some of the seasoned fries from Ken's plate after she'd polished off her own.

They saw a few other couples passing by and seated at tables around the room. The clientele provided an interesting opportunity for people-watching. "Now, do you think they're celebrating their fiftieth wedding anniversary, or are they really on their honeymoon?" Pamela gave a surreptitious nod toward an elderly couple, neither of whom probably stood taller than five feet. They were utterly engrossed in one another and she saw the man lean over to pinch the woman's thigh more than once during their lunch.

"Probably swingers. Shameless strangers on a hot, sexual honeymoon together. Like us," Ken replied with a grin.

"Now there's a picture," she said with a rueful grin. "But that's not us anymore, remember? Unless you want to change the game plan." Pamela heard a teeny hopeful note in her own voice and quickly shook her head. "No, no, I didn't mean that."

He shrugged. "Yes, you did."

"Okay, I did," she said as she lifted a glass of water to her lips and sipped from it.

Before he could reply, they were distracted by the arrival of another couple. A young man in a black leather jacket and his obviously pregnant dining companion took a seat at the next table, and immediately began making out over the bread basket. Pamela had to bite the inside of her cheek to prevent a laugh as the two of them exchanged loud, slurpy kisses and called each other nauseatingly cute pet names.

A mischievous twinkle shone in Ken's eyes as he asked, "Ready to go honey bunny?"

"You bet, cootchie-pie."

THEY NEVER DID make it to the game room that first day, instead finding things to do outside. Though he'd never been on a horse before, Ken let Pamela talk him into going for a guided ride up some of the trails near the resort. He hadn't wanted to, mainly because he was a city boy and didn't at all understand the appeal of getting his nuts crushed on the back of a bouncy animal. But her grin and the sparkle in her brown eyes were so engaging, he relented.

The hotel even provided a picnic snack, complete with champagne and caviar. Their guide presented the basket to them in a secluded wooded area an hour into the ride. The man told them he'd give them time to eat in private, and left.

"I think we're supposed to believe he's really gone and get naked," Pamela said as she passed over the caviar and nibbled on some crackers.

"Bet he had a video camera in that saddle bag."

"And I'll bet he's standing about fifty feet away hiding behind a tree."

"Poor guy. Just his bad luck to get us for his customers today," Ken said.

"Yeah, if only he'd had Mr. and Mrs. Geriatric. They'd probably have given him quite a show."

He grimaced. "I think I've lost my appetite."

"Hey, I think it's wonderful that they're obviously so mad for each other, even if they are pushing one hundred."

"You're right," he conceded. "But it's not exactly something I'd like to visualize."

No, if he was going to visualize anyone rolling around naked on the soft carpet of pine needles and old leaves beneath them, it was he and Pamela. He'd like nothing more than to pull off her clothes, uncovering her pale body in the bright sunlight. Then he'd make love to her for hours under the canopy of trees and glimpses of bright blue, cloudless sky.

It had been a grand total of about six hours since

they'd decided to back off on the physical feelings they had for one another. Six agonizing hours of heightened awareness, reaction to her smile, her laugh, her warm, sweet, citrusy scent and every breath she took.

How in heaven's name was he going to be able to stand days of it? Falling deeper for her, getting caught up in her infectious laugh, liking her more and more...yet not touching her the way he really wanted to? He wasn't a damn saint. He did, however, have a feeling that after a few more days, he was going to be completely insane.

That night they went to Reno and discovered they shared a disinterest in gambling. They lost about thirty bucks between them playing slot machines, grew bored and went to a show instead. Afterward, they discovered a great Thai restaurant, both relieved to finally eat a meal that didn't, in some way, include an aphrodisiac.

They spent the next few days in much the same way. Boating, swimming, hiking or bicycling during the day. Discovering the charm of nearby small towns, with their quaint shopping areas, restaurants and friendly residents. They laughed and held hands, talked endlessly, sometimes kissed with a sweetness that left Pamela breathless and slightly teary-eyed.

By unspoken consent they left the hotel in the evenings. Neither thought they needed any more of the carnal atmosphere at The Little Love Nest just before the uncomfortable moments when they went to bed for the night.

"I'll take the chaise lounge," Pamela said the first

night. Ken had just pulled a pillow and blanket off the round bed and prepared to sleep on the chair.

"I'll be fine," he insisted. "Less chance of falling off this thing than those silk sheets."

She gave him a sultry smile and pointed toward the velvet ropes attached to the chaise. "You could always tie yourself down on that, too."

He glared.

"I'd be happy to help."

Then he threw the pillow across the room at her.

Laughing, she tossed it back and pulled down the covers on the bed. "We could share the bed," Pamela said. "I mean we had a long, busy day. We both know the ground rules. We've gone at least the past twelve hours or so without any serious groping."

He gave her a look that was purely incredulous. "And you really think we could get through the night together in that torture device without anything happening?"

She thought about it, pictured their limbs wrapping around each other in the night, their bodies acting on instinct and suppressed desire, doing what their minds had been denying them all day. "Guess not," she said, her voice barely a whisper.

He slept on the chaise that first night and the two that followed, finally allowing her to insist that he take the bed the fourth night.

And throughout every long, sleepless minute of each long, sleepless hour, Pamela wished she had the nerve to sneak across the room, slide under the covers and cocoon herself in his arms.

It wasn't supposed to be this way. "It's too good to be true," she whispered to herself in the dark as she tried once more to count sheep in a vain effort to find sleep.

This trip was originally supposed to be about sex. It was meant to be a carnal interlude, easily indulged, joyously decadent. Sex with a stranger, fulfillment of every sensual urge, a hot-blooded affair to long remember and never regret.

It wasn't supposed to be about laughter. And friendship. Bright smiles and shared memories. Whispers and entwined fingers. Though she'd sensed she could care for the man, when she'd set out on this trip with him she hadn't imagined she would truly fall in love with him. Even the other morning, when she'd agreed to take the heat down a level and let them get to know each other, she hadn't imagined how helplessly, crazy in love with him she'd be just a few days later.

She was, though. She tried to analyze that love, tried to understand how she could be certain of it, given her history and her relationship with Peter. It was just... there. In the smile that crossed her lips when she said his name, in the pounding of her heart when he took her hand. In the delight she got watching him sleep, the low red embers of the fireplace casting shadows across his body in the bed a few feet away.

She loved being with him, admired his intelligence, loved hearing him talk about his sisters, and his business. Loved debating sports and politics with him. But it was deeper than that. She trusted him, physically, mentally, emotionally. She sensed he would be incapable of hurting her. And she knew deep in her heart that she would never be able to do anything that would hurt him.

So was that love? Yes. She truly believed it was.

Not that being in love meant she didn't mind sex being out of the picture. On the contrary, the harder she fell for him, the more she wanted him! Late Saturday night had been about pure heat. Maybe love had been blooming somewhere deep inside even then, but it hadn't been much on her mind. Emotion didn't have as much to do with those intoxicating moments in the shower as pure, undiluted lust. And it had been utterly fabulous.

So, with her emotions engaged, how might he make her feel *now*? How deeply might she lose herself in him now that he had her heart as well as her body?

She wanted to find out. Very, very soon.

9

"READY FOR BREAKFAST?"

Pamela had just exited the bathroom and was toweling her hair dry Thursday morning. As usual, they were both up early. She wondered if his night had been as sleepless as hers.

"Gimme ten," she replied.

He nodded, obviously knowing she meant it. Ken had told her more than once how much he admired her nongirliness. If she said she would be ready in ten minutes, she was. He liked that she was opinionated, told her it was refreshing that she went with her gut instincts more than her brain most times.

Peter had never told her that. Actually, no one had ever told her that.

As she finished pulling on some clothes and putting on a little lipstick, her minimum makeup requirement for being seen in public even at 8:00 a.m., the phone rang.

"It's LaVyrle," Ken said after he answered the phone.

She wondered why her coworker would be tracking her down at Lake Tahoe. Knowing LaVyrle would want an explanation as to why a man was answering her phone, Pamela shrugged. "Why don't you go ahead to the restaurant without me? I'll meet you in a few minutes, okay?"

Nodding his agreement, Ken pressed a quick kiss on her lips. "Coffee, cream no sugar. Fruit plate, wheat toast, one scrambled on the side."

She grinned. "Okay, so I'm predictable. Maybe I'll go for the English Muffin today instead!"

"No, you won't." Ken winked as he left the room, giving her privacy to take the call. She was still smiling at how well he already knew her as she answered.

"Okay, who's the dude?" That was LaVyrle. No beating around the bush.

"Uh, would you believe the bellhop?"

"Uh-uh."

"Waiter."

"Try again."

"A gorgeous hunk of male that I picked up on a beach, talked into coming with me on this trip and have fallen head over heels, madly, passionately in love with?"

A ten-second silence was followed by a bellow of LaVyrle's warm laughter. "I'll take number three."

"Me, too."

Pamela gave LaVyrle a quick rundown of her meeting with Ken, answering her friend's suspicious questions to assure her that, no, Ken was not a psycho serial killer nor a gigolo trying to con her for money. Finally, she convinced her friend that she'd simply had the great, incredible fortune to meet that rarest of breeds: a truly nice guy. A hunky, sexy, kissable, well-endowed adorable guy who loved long, slow kisses and shattering sex in hot, steamy showers. Not that she actually went into the well-endowed part. Or the sex in the shower part.

But LaVyrle could read between the lines.

"You using protection?"

Pamela didn't take offense, since that was a standard question where the two of them worked. "That's not really necessary, at this particular time, but yes, we did when it was required."

"What do you mean *not* necessary? You having a hot and wild affair or not?"

"Well, yes. But there's no sex involved."

Though LaVyrle dropped the phone, Pamela still heard her shriek of dismay. When the other woman picked up the receiver again, she said, "Tell me you did not end up with another man who doesn't like sex."

A warm smile of memory crossed her lips. "Oh, there's not a doubt in my mind that he likes sex."

He'd have to in order to be so darn good at it!

"Then tell me you didn't end up with another man who's making you doubt yourself. Honey, you have been there, done that and sent back the postcard."

She chuckled. "Don't worry, LaVyrle. There's no question of the attraction, really. There are other, uh, issues. We're slowing it down."

"Well, don't slow down too far, missy. You're coming home in two days."

"I know." A smile crossed her lips as she glanced at the thick, white rug, the tub, the round bed and the mirrors. "It'd be a shame to leave here without really experiencing all this place has to offer."

She hoped she and Ken would have at least a day or two at the end of the trip to take advantage of the possibilities. She knew she wasn't going to be able to go much longer without having him again. And she could tell by the way his dark, heavy-lidded eyes devoured her lately—her lips, her throat, her body—that he couldn't wait either.

"So was there a reason you called this morning? Is everything okay there? You haven't heard from my father, have you?"

"Not a peep here," LaVyrle replied. "Your friend Sue stopped by and asked if we'd heard from you, though. She said your father has phoned her once or twice to ask if you've called. Since Sue knew I'd seen you before you left for your trip, she told him that much, that you were okay and you'd gone out of town for a while. That's it."

"Good."

"Maybe not so good."

"Why not?"

"Well, Peter's been working on Sue, too."

She groaned. "Peter?"

"He's gone to see her, certain she knows where you are. She hasn't told but, you know, that friend of yours has a big ole heart, but not much in the way of backbone."

Pamela thought about it. "Not a huge deal, LaVyrle. Even if Sue told Peter I'd come to Tahoe, he wouldn't be able to find me. He had no idea where we were staying."

"Okay, just wanted to warn ya. So far, it's not a problem, Sue swears she won't tell. But I thought you should know that the snake's tearin' up Miami looking for you, telling everyone he needs to straighten out the big misunderstanding.'' LaVyrle snorted in disgust. "I'd like to straighten that boy out—with a tire iron."

Pamela chuckled in spite of herself. Though, thinking about it, she really didn't wish any harm on the man. She felt nothing as she thought about him. Nothing but relief. He'd been a bastard and a louse, but she'd escaped from their relationship unscathed, even the better for it. Because if it hadn't been for Peter, she'd never have met Ken that night on the beach. So, while she wasn't nearly ready to forgive and forget, she didn't feel the need to expend energy in hating him, either.

After chatting with LaVyrle for a few minutes about how things were going at the center, Pamela ended the call and left the room. She took her time walking to the restaurant, pausing along the way for a closer look at some of the statues in the corridor. Ken had hurried her past them every other time they'd walked by.

Damn, before they left this place, she was determined to figure out what Miss Mona had meant when she'd said it was good that Pamela was tall.

As soon as she entered the restaurant, she spotted Ken sitting at a table in a corner. He saw her, stood, waved, then froze.

''Ken!''

Pamela hadn't said his name. Someone directly behind her had. A female someone. Slowly, Pamela turned on her heel and looked at the woman standing there.

''My gosh, Ken, is that you?'' the other woman said as

she pushed past Pamela and walked across the restaurant to give Ken a big, friendly hug.

Pamela watched as Ken held himself stiff beneath the woman's embrace. He caught her eye over the blonde's head, and she almost chuckled at the look of horrified helplessness on his face. Okay, so he wasn't entirely glad to see this person. That was a good thing, considering she sure seemed enthusiastic about seeing him!

Taking her time, Pamela crossed the room to join them, studying the newcomer as she approached. She was little. Teeny, bubbly and blond. Just the kind of rah-rah-cheerleader twit Pamela had so disliked in high school. The kind of female who always made Pamela feel huge and Amazonian, who'd always brought curling irons to keep in their gym lockers at school so they could look perfect after an icky, sweaty, nasty old game of softball.

"What a surprise! I was just thinking of you the other day," the woman was saying as Pamela stepped up behind her. "I never expected to run into you *here*, of all places."

"Hello, Liz. Yes, this is a surprise for me, too."

Liz? As in ex-girlfriend Liz? Pamela's teeth clenched even tighter in her jaw. What were the odds they'd run into his ex-girlfriend in this place? There had to be a million other honeymoon resorts in the country. Okay, so maybe The Little Love Nest was showing up in feature ads in the back of every bridal magazine on the planet, but couldn't Liz have chosen the Caribbean? The French Riviera? The moon?

As if it wasn't bad enough that Ken's ex had shown

up here—did she really have to look like the same kind of Kewpie doll cutie that always made Pamela feel huge and bumbling? *Well, doesn't this just stink!*

"Dave and I went around in circles for months planning our wedding. Finally we got tired of it, hopped a flight to Vegas and got married." The woman laughed, the sound grating on Pamela's nerves like nails on a chalkboard. "We'd seen all the ads for this place, found out they had a last-minute cancellation, and came up last night."

"Small world," Ken said weakly as he finally pulled away and disentangled Liz's arm from around his waist. He took a single step back, unable to go farther since he was blocked by the table. Shooting Pamela a look that promised an explanation, he crossed his arms and turned his attention toward his ex.

"So why are *you* here?" Liz asked, completely oblivious to the fact that Pamela was staring down at the top of her head, noting that her dark roots were within a week of needing a color job. "Goodness, Ken, you didn't follow me, did you? I mean, we broke up months and months ago!"

Kewpie-face might not have noticed, her being so low to the ground and all, but Pamela definitely saw Ken roll his eyes. His lips twitched, and she wondered at his good humor, considering the woman had implied he was stalking her.

"Liz, I've been here since Saturday. I had no idea you'd turn up. Congratulations on your marriage. Where's the groom?"

"He's making arrangements for a hiking trip this afternoon."

For the first time, Pamela heard a bit of the chirpy good humor fade from the other woman's voice.

"Still a real outdoorsman, hm?" Ken asked, his tone sympathetic.

"That's why we had such a problem planning the wedding," the woman admitted. "Couldn't interfere with hunting, skiing or boating seasons. Anyway, why are you here? Are you doing a software project for the hotel?"

"What makes you think I'm not here on my honeymoon?"

The woman laughed again. "Oh, you big silly, I know you haven't been dating anyone since me. I bump into Diana occasionally. She keeps me updated."

Diana? Oh, one of his sisters. Well, maybe Ken could afford to be magnanimous, amused in the face of her sweetly spoken put-downs, but Pamela had had quite enough.

"Darling, I'm *so* sorry I kept you waiting. It took forever to shower and get all that body paint off from last night," Pamela said as she stepped around Ken's ex. "That Cherry Jubilee flavor might have been tasty, but it leaves bright red stains in the most *embarrassing* places!" Ignoring his widened eyes, she slipped her arms around his neck and planted a long, wet kiss on his parted lips.

She sort of forgot about Liz at that point. So did Ken, apparently. Because for several long moments he kissed her senseless, coaxing needy shivers out of her with his lips and the slow, sweet strokes of his tongue.

Oh, it had been too long since he'd kissed her like this! They'd both tried so hard to avoid physical contact in the past few days. That had done nothing but banked the fire! Time certainly hadn't doused it. Because now, in his arms, with his mouth on hers, she found herself jolted back to that steamy shower, feeling the water pelt her, smelling his hot desire, experiencing his kisses clear down to her toes.

"Ahem."

She was the one who ended the kiss. It hurt, but she did it, knowing they had an audience. Not that most of the patrons in The Little Love Nest's restaurant were going to be too shocked by a couple kissing. She and Ken had seen even more intimate moments, particularly between the eight-and-a-half-months pregnant bride and her Rebel-Without-a-Clue hubby, who seemed to have made it their mission to play tonsil hockey in public at least ten times an hour.

"Sorry," Pamela whispered against Ken's lips as she finally ended the kiss. "I couldn't resist."

His breathing was almost as ragged as hers, his eyes glazed. "Forgiven."

"I've missed you," she said softly, knowing he understood what she meant. *I've missed this.*

"Me, too."

Before she could ask what they were going to do about it, Liz interrupted. "Are you going to introduce me?"

Pamela finally glanced at the blonde, who watched

them with a speculative look on her face. "Hello, I'm Pamela." She did not offer any last name. She certainly wasn't going to introduce herself as Ken's wife. Not when this woman was obviously a friend of Ken's family. She could only imagine the kind of turmoil that would cause if word got back to his sisters or parents that he'd gotten married without telling anyone!

"How nice to meet you," the woman said, sounding confused but not malicious. "I didn't realize Ken was *with* someone."

Pamela heard the woman's real meaning—she didn't realize Ken was *seeing* someone—but feigned ignorance. "It'd be kind of a bummer to stay here alone," Pamela commented. She heard Ken's chuckle.

"So, the two of you are, uh..."

"Vacationing," Ken supplied.

Pamela could tell the woman was dying to ask more questions. She waited, expectantly, but didn't pry. Pamela had to give her credit for that. Okay, so she wasn't a complete bimbo. She did have a little tact.

"Well, I'm very happy to meet you," Liz finally said when she realized no explanation was forthcoming. "You're lucky—Ken's an amazing man."

She again caught a note of wistfulness in the other woman's voice and wondered at it. Perhaps she had regrets? From the sound of things, her husband wasn't exactly the type to sweep a girl off her feet with grand romantic gestures—unless they involved camping gear or fishing poles.

But Ken...well, Ken was the kind of man who'd cover a woman with his jacket. Kiss her within an inch of her life. Tuck her into bed alone. Rescue a bound-for-the-fireplace wedding gown. Go on a honeymoon with a stranger. Make love to her until she nearly fainted with pleasure. Then gently insist they get to know each other better.

That was Ken. *Her* Ken. She curled closer to him, sliding her hand around his waist and resting her head on his shoulder. When he pressed a soft kiss to her temple, she sighed with pleasure. Not for Liz's benefit. No, the pleasure was all Pamela's.

The other woman watched for a moment, then glanced away.

"Well, I'd better see what's holding up my husband," Liz said as she turned to leave. Just then, a good-looking, beefy blond man entered the room and waved. Liz smiled and waved back.

"Here he is now! I have been wanting him to meet you," she told Ken.

Pamela heard Ken's nearly inaudible groan. Great. First the ex, now the guy the ex had dumped him for. She wished they'd had breakfast in their room. Actually, she wished they'd had breakfast in bed. The same bed. Together.

"Tomorrow," she murmured, deciding right then and there that the platonic part of their honeymoon was *over*.

Four days. She'd given him four days, more than half their vacation. She'd suppressed the desires and the needs, given them the chance to get to know one another. Now she was certain, one hundred percent convinced that she was crazy about the guy, would have been crazy about him even if Peter Weiss had never been in her life. This was no rebound. This was not about wounded feelings, nor about a virgin dying to be deflowered.

This was about her, Pamela the woman, wanting to be with Ken, the man she'd fallen in love with. Period. And it was about damn time she let him know that, too. But first...there was the ex to deal with.

If Dave knew Liz had been dating Ken the previous year, he certainly didn't appear to hold a grudge as he joined them and extended his hand in greeting. Somehow Liz managed to get them all to agree to have breakfast together. It should have been a miserably uncomfortable meal, but Liz actually proved to be a nice, blond Kewpie doll. Okay, she wasn't someone Pamela would normally have wanted for a friend, but she was funny and warm. She seemed genuinely happy that Ken had moved on with his life, though Pamela couldn't help noticing how closely she watched every time Ken took Pamela's hand or pushed an errant lock of hair off her brow.

Dave was a blustery, big-hearted, down-to-earth guy. He and Liz had apparently been high-school sweethearts. While he obviously adored her, it was equally apparent he was not exactly skilled in romance. Here he was on his honeymoon discussing the best fishing tackle, the weight room, and inviting Ken and Pamela to come along on their five-hour hike that afternoon.

"No, thanks ever so much, Dave, but I think I feel a bit of a cold coming on. I'm counting on Ken to *take* care of me today. In our room."

She heard him suck in a breath and knew he was fully aware of what she was really saying.

"You will take care of me, darling, won't you?" she asked, glancing at Ken. He met her stare, held it, incinerated it. Then he smiled that slow grin and looked away without saying a word. But his hand tightened in hers, his body shifted closer.

He hadn't been touching her any more during breakfast than he had been in the past few days, but every brush of his fingers sent shivers down her spine. She couldn't stop thinking of that kiss. The awareness was back, thrumming between them, as vibrant and alive now as it had been Saturday. He felt it too; she could tell. His posture was relaxed, but his body was tense and alert next to hers. When she shifted on the bench seat and brushed her hip against his, he hissed and jerked upward.

Oh, boy.

"Besides," Pamela continued, knowing Ken was listening intently, "Ken and I only have a few more days before we have to return to Florida. And I think I'd rather stay here and experience more of the hotel's *amenities.*"

"Sounds lovely," Liz said softly.

"Nah, boring," Dave said with a laugh. "We can laze around at home. We're on vacation—we've gotta go do stuff!" Liz's sigh turned into a smile when her husband threw his arm around her shoulder and tugged her close to nuzzle the top of her head.

As they finished breakfast and lingered over coffee, Pamela began itching to get away. She wanted nothing more than to return to their room so she could see if Ken was as ready to end this platonic situation as she was. "You know, I just remembered I have to make a call. Sweetie, why don't you finish your coffee and come back to the room when you're done?"

The other two were oblivious to the undercurrents running between them, but Ken's eyes brightened and a slow smile crossed his lips. "Okay. But, uh, after you finish your phone call, there's something we need to talk about."

Giving him a distracted nod, she leaned over to press a quick kiss on his cheek. She had to give him credit. He didn't so much as wince when she nibbled his earlobe.

She wasn't quite so controlled. When he responded by slipping his hand between her thighs, she gasped. He smiled as he gently caressed the bare skin along the hem of her khaki shorts. Finally noticing the other couple watching them curiously, she stood up on shaky legs.

"It was great meeting you. Maybe we'll see you again before we leave," she said, trying to sound normal, trying to hide the fact that Ken's touch had stolen every thought from her brain and the breath from her lungs.

"Oh, sure," Dave replied. "Let's plan on doing lots of things together. It's more fun with another couple. You know, when your cold's gone."

"We'll see," she replied. Then she gave Ken a purely evil look. "We might be pretty *tied up* these next few days."

This time she got a reaction. Ken cocked his head to the side and narrowed his eyes, obviously remembering the velvet ropes in their room. "Yes, absolutely. Though I do find I've developed a real desire to do some *riding*."

As her legs turned to jelly, Pamela grabbed the back of the chair she'd just vacated. She wondered if anyone noticed the wobble in her walk as she exited the restaurant. She didn't really care. Nor did she care that a passing maid watched as she danced a little jig around one of the cheesy sex statues in the lobby, then dashed toward their room like she was doing a full court press.

Minutes. She only had a few minutes until Ken arrived. She wanted to be ready. Everything had to be just right.

KEN DIDN'T WANT another cup of coffee. He could have left when Pamela did. He certainly didn't feel the need to sit here and make small talk with Liz and Dave. No, sitting across from his ex-girlfriend and her new husband wasn't the worst breakfast he'd ever had, but he couldn't say it was high up on his list of fun things to do on one's honeymoon. Not that he was really on his honeymoon.

So no, it wasn't the company, nor was it the coffee that kept him from returning to their room. It wasn't Pamela's phone call, either, which he suspected she'd made up.

He was stalling. Somehow, he felt like a kid preparing for the last week of school, with final exams to get through before a long, glorious summer filled with decadent freedom.

Only, he didn't have a final exam, he had a conversation to get through. An explanation. An apology. Hopefully it wouldn't be a *final* in any way. Then, if he was very lucky, they could proceed to the long, glorious part.

The past four days had been delightful, filled with laughter and smiles, deep conversations and a growing sense of emotion. Definitely emotion. And he wanted more of that. Much, much more. Beyond this week, beyond this month. Enough to last a lifetime.

Ken tried to work up some anger at himself for doing exactly what he'd sworn he would not do—falling in love with Pamela Bradford. Too late.

As he'd suspected the first time he'd seen her, the first time her father had spoken of her, he found Pamela Bradford irresistible. She was funny and tough. Sexy and vulnerable. Thoughtful and outrageous. A beguiling blend of temptress and virgin.

He'd planned to wait until they returned to Florida to tell her the truth about why he'd come with her—that he'd been at the bachelor party and her father had asked him to look after her. Now, however, he knew he couldn't wait. Because he sensed he wasn't alone in his feelings. Pamela had fallen, too. Fallen damn hard. He felt sure she knew him enough, trusted him enough, that she would believe him when he told her how sorry he was for not being honest with her. The longer he delayed, the worse he felt.

Truthfully, he also didn't think he could wait until they were back in Miami to make love to her again. Not now. Not when he knew how he felt about her, and was certain she returned his feelings.

So, the time had come to wipe the slate clean—which was why he lingered over an additional cup of coffee he didn't want, chatted with an ex-girlfriend who bored him, and listened to Dave's explanation of the benefits of ice fishing to a man's prostate.

He hadn't noticed that an hour had passed until a waiter handed him a note. "From your room," the young man whispered.

Ken glanced at it, noted Pamela's writing, and opened the page.

Come *now* unless you want me to start without you.

His hand shook and he dropped the paper, watching it flutter to the floor. Time to go.

Quickly saying goodbye to Liz and Dave, he made his way out of the restaurant. He didn't know what to expect. The virgin? The seductress? The basketball nut? He was still asking himself that question when he entered their room, pushed the door closed behind him, and spotted her.

The vamp.

"Black leather," he murmured, his voice caressing the words as his gaze traveled over every inch of her.

She lay on the thick white rug, bathed in the morning sunlight that spilled forth from the half-opened patio blinds. Her hair was loose, falling in a mass of waves to below her bare shoulders. Her chestnut curls were rich and vibrant against the rug and the thick fluffy pillows on which she reclined.

When he'd gathered the strength, he dropped his gaze lower. Down the long, smooth column of her neck, the gentle, kissable flesh of her nape. To the soft pale curves of her breasts, pushed temptingly high by the black top she wore. He thought it was called a bustier. One of those Madonna things with leather and metal loops. It cinched tight around her midriff, tighter beneath her full breasts, leaving them exposed almost to the nipples. A shiny black ribbon laced up the front, holding the whole thing together.

He wanted to undo it with his teeth.

He also wanted to explore that tempting strip of skin between the bottom of the bustier and the elastic band holding up the ridiculously tiny black panties she wore.

Her bare legs went on for days, from sweetly curved hips all the way down to a pair of spiked black high heels that adorned her feet. She shifted under his stare, moving restlessly against the fur. He saw her mouth open on a sigh at the physical sensations bombarding her and marveled at Pamela's sensuous nature.

He took a deep breath, shuddering with the effort. "You didn't start without me?" he finally asked as he made his feet move across the room toward her.

She answered in a sultry purr. "Did you want me to?"

That would be lovely to see. Pamela pleasuring herself, touching her body, showing him what she liked. "Another time. Definitely."

She smiled a slow, knowing smile, obviously aware

that his restraint was nearly gone. If she so much as lifted her hair off her bare shoulder he might just lose it then and there.

She held out a hand for him to join her on the rug. "It took you long enough."

He could hardly remember why. Why on earth had he delayed coming here to find her like this? Then he remembered. Their conversation. The big one. He'd completely forgotten it the second he'd spotted her. "I really did want to talk to you." He cleared his throat and tried to focus. "Have a serious talk with you."

She shook her head. "No talking. We've talked enough over the past four days."

"Pamela..."

"Later, Ken. We'll talk later. About anything you want. Right now the only talking I want is you telling me how much you want to be inside me and me telling you that if I don't feel your naked body against mine soon I'm going to go completely insane."

As Pamela rose to her knees in front of him, giving him a clear view right down the top of her minuscule black leather outfit, he gave up all thought of conversation. There was only now, only this. For the first time in his life he was going to make love to a woman he really loved.

Everything else would come later.

She dropped her head back, looked up at him with a smile full of mystery and promise. "Now, *you*, get that off," she said, pointing to his shirt.

Remembering ordering her to do much the same thing Saturday night, Ken grinned. His grin faded as she reached for his belt buckle. She brushed his hands aside when he moved to undo it himself, so he pulled his shirt off instead. He had just dropped it to the floor as Pamela undid his trousers and pushed them down his hips. She gave a throaty little sigh of approval as she trailed her fingers across his erection, which strained against the front of his tight boxer-briefs.

"As I recall, we were interrupted Saturday night," she said huskily. Before he could reply, she'd freed him from his briefs and moved her sweet wet mouth over him.

Pamela was acting on instinct and desire, becoming the sensual person she'd kept buried all her life. Certainly she'd never done *this* before. She worried for an instant that she'd be clumsy, but could tell by the way Ken's breath grew choppy and hoarse that she was doing all right. She liked the musky taste of him, the feel of his hands tangling in her hair, the sounds he made. But he wouldn't let her go on too long.

"Can't take much of that, sweetheart," he said as he gently pulled away from her and kicked off the last of his clothing.

She still knelt below him, certain she'd never seen a more perfect man, a more beautiful male body. All deliciously hers. Every ounce of pent-up passion and desire she'd ever experienced rushed through her with the speed and velocity of a freight train. She tingled down to her fingertips. Like a starving person at a banquet, she wanted to try it all, sample everything.

Mostly she wanted his mouth. His sweet-talking mouth. When he dropped to his knees and knelt before her, catching her lips in a kiss that went on forever, she almost cried at how right it felt.

"I'm in love with you. You know that, don't you?" he said against her lips as he lowered her to the rug.

"I know," she managed to say, through her sighs and her tears and the pounding of her heart. "I'm in love with you, too. I think I started loving you the moment you handed me your jacket that first night on the beach."

"It's crazy," he whispered. "This is exactly what I swore wasn't going to happen. But I've never felt anything was more right in my life."

He moved his mouth lower, pressing hot kisses on the curves of her breasts. But not low enough. She arched her back, offering herself to him. Wanting more.

He took what she offered, tugging at the satiny lace between her breasts with his teeth. Untying her. Exposing her. Then he stared down at her, his eyes getting heavy and dark before he lowered his head again to take one nipple completely in his mouth. He moved lower, pressing kisses across her chest, her belly, paying careful attention to her other breast.

Pamela shrugged the bustier completely off. Running her flat palm across her stomach, she noted the way his lips parted as he watched her touch herself. He couldn't tear his gaze away as she moved her hand lower, brushing the edge of the tiny black panties. The nylon fabric slipped down, revealing the dark curls between her legs. Ken groaned at the sight.

She liked this sense of intimate power, this sensuality

she was able to share with him. She knew she was safe to explore anything. Everything.

Reaching over to the fireplace hearth, she retrieved a small bottle. "I found these in the bathroom," she said with a purr. "This mountain air has dried out my skin. Would you mind?"

The hotel had provided a variety of scented oils, guaranteed perfect for sensuous massage. She could think of nothing more pleasureful or sensuous than the feel of Ken's hands touching every inch of her. As she fully intended to do to him.

Giving him an innocent smile, she handed him the plastic bottle, then settled back on the rug. She stretched against the faux fur, the softness bringing heightened awareness to her already electrified skin.

"It would be my pleasure," he said throatily as he took the bottle and opened the cap. He lifted it and sniffed. "Nice."

"It's called 'New Orleans Evening.' Plumeria. And the tiniest bit of sandalwood. It says that's an aphrodisiac."

"I don't think we need it," Ken said as he poured a small amount into his hands and lowered the bottle to the floor.

Then he moved his hands to her shoulders, smoothing the liquid over her skin. The warmth of his fingers and the slickness of the light oil made his every movement a seductive delight. His hands didn't so much touch as glide across her, heightening her anticipation, bringing her nerve endings roaring to life. The sweet scent filled her brain and made her think of lying in a garden courtyard, under an endless navy-blue night sky, surrounded by the fragrance of heady flowers and by warmth. And by love.

His hands touched every inch of her, making her want to weep with the pleasure of sensation. Looking up at his passion-filled face, surrounded by his scent, the jagged sound of her own breathing and the rapid staccato beat of her heart, she felt more in tune to her senses than she ever had in her life.

"I could touch you for days."

"I want you inside me," she said hoarsely. He slipped his hand between her thighs, pulling the panties off and tossing them aside. Stroking her expertly, he slid one finger into her body as he lowered his mouth to hers for another of those deep, wet kisses. When he flicked the pad of his thumb higher, against her most sensitive spot, she cried out, her hips bucking up in response. "Now, Ken, please."

He grabbed one of the condoms she'd left near the massage oil, put it on and moved over her. Her body was still slick; not greasy, but moist and fragrant. Open and ready for him. She cupped his face in her hands as he slid into her, filling her up. No pain this time. Just sweet, gentle possession.

If Saturday night had been about elemental need and soul-consuming lust, this was about all the other aspects of lovemaking. Desire, yes. Physical arousal, oh, absolutely. But there was such tenderness, such passion. Each of them moved together like two parts of the same person, anticipating each stroke, tailoring every movement to suit one another. Climbing higher, building the pleasure, until Pamela simply had to cry out with it.

He caught her cries with his lips, then increased the pace. Pamela wrapped her legs around him, not even noticing at first when he pushed one leg higher, so it slid over his shoulder. When he plunged back into her, she gasped at how deep he was. She caught his movements, met them, danced to the crazy-sweet rhythm only the two of them could hear.

And as they came together, she knew this man was a part of her in every way. Not for a week. Not for a fling or a mindless sexual release. This man was her soul mate.

She knew it. In her heart she'd always known it.

10

"SHOW ME WHAT Miss Mona meant when she said it's good that I'm tall."

If Ken hadn't already lowered Pamela into the hot bubbly water of the whirlpool, he might have dropped her. Instead, he shook his head and eased himself in next to her. "We'd drown."

She splashed water in his face, then curled her wet naked body up against his. "I meant later."

Though it had only been a half hour since they'd made love on the white rug inside, he found himself reacting physically to her suggestion. No question, Pamela was open to exploring her own sexuality, and he looked forward to showing her what she wanted to know. He'd been thinking of exactly that when she'd taken him into her mouth earlier. The thought made him groan. "Later."

Pamela shifted on the seat, dropping lower until her shoulders were covered, obviously enjoying the heat and the bubbles swirling around them in the fragrant spa. "I can hardly wait," she murmured. "For everything."

"I think I've created a monster," he said with a chuckle. "I don't know if I'm going to be able to keep up with you."

"You're doing okay so far," she said as she slid closer. When she turned to face him, then moved one thigh across his lap to straddle him, she obviously felt his renewed interest. "I'd say you're doing just fine."

Unable to resist the sweet, sultry challenge in her voice, he slipped his hands into her hair, pulling her closer. Her eyes widened as he caught her mouth in a hot, wet kiss that left them both panting.

"Do you want to go back inside now?" he asked, his voice husky. Though the hot tub was relaxing, he wanted nothing more than to take her to bed and make love to her again.

"This patio is *very* private. I think that's the point—we can do anything we like," she said as she tilted her hips closer.

She was on top of him, her flesh teasing his beneath the water and Ken *so* wanted to slide up into her swollen heat.

"Might be nice to make love in a bed for a change," he said hoarsely. "Besides, we didn't bring anything from inside. For protection."

A tiny pout pulled at her lips. "You're right. But it's just so nice out here. So warm and wet."

He groaned as she wiggled again. She moved closer, taking the tip of his erection into her body, but no more. Bracing her hands on the back of the hot tub behind his head, she held herself just above him. Ken couldn't resist her bare breasts, inches from his mouth, and allowed himself a pleasureful kiss. His body was screaming at him to thrust up into her, filling her completely, but he resisted. "Pamela, let's take this inside. I want to protect you."

"Have you had many lovers?" she asked, looking down at him with both curiosity and dread.

"That's a helluva question to ask at a time like this," he managed to grit out, holding on to the thin thread of his sanity as she swayed just above him.

"You know I haven't," she prodded. "I'm safe. And I have the feeling you're not the type to play the field, so I suspect you're healthy, too."

He knew what she was getting at. "Don't worry, Pamela, I'm fine. There are, however, other issues. Small, screaming, diaper-wetting ones."

She chuckled, lowered herself a little, drawing a groan from his mouth. "You're killing me," he muttered.

"Don't you like babies?" she asked, her tone growing more serious.

Babies? Their babies? Somehow, while the idea should have left him feeling *deflated*, he felt warmly confident instead. "Yes, sweetheart. I do. But how about we finish the honeymoon, then maybe go on a date or two before we think about naming our children, okay?"

She sighed and lifted herself off him. "All right. You win." She smiled gently. "I'm glad, though."

"About what?"

"That you like children. I do, too."

He knew she was referring to the future. Their future. Their happily ever after future. "We're talking the SUV and the two-point-five here, aren't we?"

She nodded.

"You sure you're ready for that?"

"We can date for the next year and I won't be any more certain than I am right now about my feelings for you." She spoke simply, her words coming from her heart.

Her honest assurance awed him. He remained silent, staring at her, wondering how on earth his life could have changed so miraculously, so fulfillingly, in just a matter of days.

Were there really such things as perfect soul mates? Had he somehow known she was his from the first time he'd seen her? Why else would she have consumed his thoughts, appealed to him so completely, brought out every protective instinct he owned from the moment they'd met?

It was as if something inside had been telling him all along that they were meant to be together. She obviously felt it, too. How rare was that? How many people had the fortune to not only meet their perfect match, but to also understand and recognize the real thing when they stumbled upon it?

"I'll be right back," she said with a flirtatious smile. "Don't you go anywhere."

She stepped out of the hot tub, gloriously naked and glistening in the morning sunlight. Grabbing a fluffy towel off a nearby chair, she wrapped it around her nude body, moving slowly as if she knew he watched.

"You sure you don't want me to come inside, too?" he asked, unable to tear his eyes from the line of her neck and the long strands of dark hair brushing the curves of her breasts. "We have yet to fool around in that round bed."

She paused, her hand on the patio door handle and raised her index finger to her mouth. Nibbling on it thoughtfully, she finally said, "That's very tempting. But how about later tonight? For now I want to be out here with you, hearing the birds, breathing the cool fresh air. There's something terribly decadent about being outside, naked, in the broad daylight, isn't there? Even if no one could possibly see?"

He nodded his agreement.

"Then again," she said with a grin, "I was practically naked on the beach the night we met."

The night they met. On the beach. He closed his eyes, remembering the conversation they were supposed to have. "Pamela, wait a minute. Before you go inside, before we, uh...well, there's something you should know about the night we met. I want to wipe the slate clean between us."

She paused, waiting.

"That first night, the night of the bachelor party. Well, it wasn't *completely* a coincidence that I found you on the beach," he said.

She raised an eyebrow, then laughed softly. "Well, of course it wasn't, silly."

He froze, wondering if she knew the truth, if she'd known all along.

"It was fate, Ken," she finally continued with a heartbreakingly sweet smile that shot through him with the power and intensity of a lightning bolt.

Her sweetness, trust and unadulterated joy touched

him someplace deep inside. Here he was, about to repay that trust by admitting he'd deceived her, even if it was out of a desire to protect her.

Ken wanted to make it up to her. Wanted to make her understand, even though he, himself, didn't fully comprehend how he could have had such strong feelings for her since before they'd even met. But it was the truth.

"It was more than fate," he finally said. "Do you believe in love at first sight?"

"Of course," she said. "Didn't I tell you that earlier? That's exactly what happened when you handed me your coat."

She bent forward and pressed a sweet kiss on his lips. "Fate." Then she ducked into the room, leaving him alone before he even had a chance to tell her.

Love at first sight and fate. Plus a bachelor party for a guy he couldn't stand with a bunch of other guys who had seen the woman he loved in a G-string and pasties.

It was time to come clean.

PAMELA PAUSED in the bathroom to brush her hair and pull it up off her face before retrieving the condoms. She'd grabbed a handful, mentally laughing at the expression she knew she'd see on his face when he saw the seven foil packets.

She'd stepped out of the bathroom, preparing to go back outside, when she heard a knock on the door. "Oh, great," she murmured, wondering who'd be bothering them, specifically since she'd hung the Do Not Disturb sign on the knob when she came back from breakfast.

The hotel did enjoy bringing little surprises to the rooms, however. Like the champagne that first night, and a decadent chocolate raspberry truffle another evening. Tempted in spite of herself, she called, "Just a minute," then grabbed a pair of Ken's sweatpants and a long T-shirt to pull over her naked body.

It was a good thing, too. Because when she opened the door and saw who stood there, she froze on the spot. If she'd been wearing nothing but a towel, she might have been startled enough to drop the thing!

"Peter?!"

"Hello, darling,"

"You are *not* here. This can't be happening."

"Can I come in?"

"No."

"Pamela, we need to talk, and I'd rather not do it out here in the hallway."

She pushed the door toward his face. "There's nothing to talk about."

He kept his foot between the door and the jamb. "Please give me five minutes."

"I'll give you a broken foot. I can't believe you followed me here."

"How could I not? Knowing you were here alone, heartbroken about our misunderstanding. I had to come, just as soon as I found out where you were."

Misunderstanding? Yeah. Sure. Right. "How did you find out?"

His eyes shifted. "Sue."

She didn't believe him. "Sue couldn't have told you where to find me because she didn't know where we were supposed to be staying. You're not very good at lying anymore, are you?"

"She told me you came to Tahoe," he admitted. "And I found out where you were staying when I found the brochures for this place." He looked around, peering around the door to the room, his eyes widening when he saw the tub, the rug, the bed. "Thinking of you here, alone, miserable and depressed, I couldn't stand it."

"The brochures? Which brochures would those be? Surely not the brochures in the desk drawer in my apartment?"

Again the eyes went down.

"That's called breaking and entering."

"No, it's called desperation. I had to find out where you were so I could explain everything."

"No, you didn't. What you have to do now is get back on a plane to Miami and never come near me again."

"Pam, baby, I can see how unhappy you are. You're a mess. Moping around in your room, looking like that."

She shouldn't have cared about his opinion, but she still crossed her arms, offended. "Looking like that?"

"You know, like you're so upset you can't even get dressed in the morning. Lying around all day, crying, not seeing anyone. It's not healthy."

"Peter, I'm going to give you one more chance to remove your foot from this door before I scream for someone to come help."

"Don't be silly. I would imagine this place is sound-proofed for screams." He gave her a lecherous look, which she supposed he intended to be sexually titillating, amusing or charming. She found it faintly disgusting.

"If I scream, it won't be a bellman who comes running. It'll be the guy in my hot tub."

He gave her a patronizing smile. "You don't have to try to save face. I already know what a fool I was to not make you see how I really feel about you. It isn't necessary to try to make me jealous."

Just then the patio door opened. She heard it from behind her, and watched as Peter's eyes widened. "Who's that?"

"The guy in my hot tub," she explained matter-of-factly.

She should probably have felt an instant of satisfaction at the look of stunned dismay on her ex-fiancé's face. Frankly, she didn't care enough about him one way or another to muster up the energy. She just regretted his intrusion, knowing if he hadn't knocked, she and Ken would have been enjoying a delicious daylight interlude right about now.

"What's keeping you, Pamela?" she heard Ken call. Turning, she saw him walk into the room from outside. Naked. Wet. Glistening. Utterly glorious. Then he noticed her standing at the door and cocked his head in confusion. When he spotted Peter, she saw him tense from several feet away.

Peter just looked stunned. He stared at Ken, shock and confusion written all over his face. Pamela had to hide a grin, knowing Ken was the kind of man who made other men feel *small*.

"McBain?" Peter said, his voice barely a whisper. "Ken McBain?"

She didn't understand. Glancing back and forth between them, she watched as Ken grabbed for a towel from the patio and slung it around his hips. Peter still looked dazed.

"What the hell are you doing here with my fiancée?"

"I'm not your fiancée," she retorted mechanically, still not quite following the conversation. These two *knew* each other?

"Pamela, what is he doing here? You're not—you didn't...." he looked around the room again, then at Ken, who still stood just inside the patio door. "Just how long has this been going on? Were you cheating on me with him even before we broke up?" Peter looked more stunned than angry. "I didn't even know you two knew each other!"

Finally, it sunk in. "I didn't know *you* two knew each other, either," she mumbled. Glancing over her shoulder at Ken, she saw a look of pleading on his face. "Ken?"

"Pamela, just shut the door and come back outside so we can talk."

"So you've been here all week?" Peter interrupted, glaring at Ken. "Of course you have. No one's seen you since the night of the party. And Jared obviously knew it. That's why he acted so funny about you being out of the office this week."

Jared? There was no denying the implication. Pamela sucked in a breath, not wanting to believe it. *Ken worked for her father?*

"Tell me it's not true," she whispered.

"Of course it's true," Peter retorted.

"You shut up," Pamela and Ken both snapped at the same time.

"Pamela, I can explain," Ken said. "Just shut the door so we can talk."

Frankly, she was getting a little sick of men telling her they could explain things away. First Peter. Now, oh, God, now Ken. She shook her head, slowly, trying to take it in.

She thought about what Peter had said, still trying to make sense of everything. Ken hadn't been seen since the night of the party. *The party? That* party? "You were there? You saw?"

He gave a single, regretful nod. "Sweetheart, my heart was breaking for you."

"What a crock. You were a wreck and he saw a chance to get into your pants," Peter said with a sneer.

This time, Pamela didn't even give him a warning. She slammed the door, hard, probably crunching a few of his toes, but at least getting rid of him. He pounded on the door a couple of times, then gave up. For all she knew, he might have been waiting right outside, listening, waiting for the argument he must have anticipated.

She couldn't argue. She couldn't muster the energy to tell Ken off, to tell him where to go.

Peter had hurt her.

Ken. Well, Ken had devastated her.

"Pamela, you've got to listen to me."

"I want you to leave me alone," she whispered.

"Pamela, it's not what you think. Yes, I was at the

party. I barely know Peter, or any of the other men who were there. I'd only been in Miami a few weeks. I was leaving as you came in. And once I saw you, saw what happened, I only wanted to help you and make sure you were all right."

He reached for her, trying to take her hand, but she yanked it away and curled her arms tightly around her body. "That's why you conveniently found me on the beach," she said softly, still reeling, feeling the same sense of betrayal she'd felt as she sat inside that stupid cake listening to her fiancé talk about why he was marrying her.

"I just wanted to make sure you got home okay."

"As a favor to my father? Your boss?"

She heard him groan. "It wasn't like that."

"Well, what was it like? Which part do I have wrong? You saw me at the most humiliating, vulnerable moment of my life. You tracked me down and took me home, then came on this trip with me. You made me fall in love with you," her voice broke and he reached for her again. Again she stepped away. "But there's one thing you didn't do. You never once bothered to mention the truth."

"I tried to tell you a little while ago."

"Better a week late than never, huh?"

"I was afraid if I told you sooner, before you got to know and trust me enough to know it *killed* me to be dishonest with you, that you'd lash out and refuse to let me help you."

"Don't you mean I'd refuse to let you into my bed?"

He cursed and ran his hands over his brow and

through his hair, still devastatingly gorgeous in nothing but the white towel, his powerful body tense and sinewy. "Don't you understand I was afraid you were going to come out here and get taken advantage of all over again?"

"Isn't that *exactly* what happened?"

He froze, looking hurt by the accusation, but she didn't relent. "Please just go away."

"Pamela, we can get past this."

She shook her head slowly. "I don't know that we can. I just want you to answer one question for me, Ken. Please, just be honest with me about one thing."

"Anything."

She caught his eye and held it, so he'd understand how important this moment was to her. To them.

"Did my father ask you to come with me on this trip?"

She saw the answer in his eyes long before it crossed his lips. And her heart broke even more, if that was humanly possible.

"Pamela, that's not why I came. He might have asked me, but…"

"Don't say another word to me. I need to be alone right now. Just please go away and let me be by myself for a while, to think about this, to try to absorb it." She was crying now, unable to stop the tears pricking the corners of her eyes. She blinked rapidly, not wanting him to see, just wanting to hold it together long enough to get him to leave her alone with her thoughts.

"Pamela, I'm in love with you," he said, a heartbreakingly tender expression on his face. "You know that.

This doesn't change how we feel about each other. I couldn't be honest with you up front and I so deeply regret that."

She shook her head, so confused and tired and overwhelmed. He was in love with her? Maybe he thought he was. Or maybe he, like Peter, was in love with the idea of a wealthy father-in-law. She just didn't know right now. It was too raw, too sudden and unexpected. She'd been on a roller-coaster ride of emotions for a week now and she honestly didn't trust her own instincts.

In a low, weary voice, she said, "Please, give me some time." Not waiting for his reply, she walked across the room and entered the bathroom, locking the door behind her.

She listened for a few minutes while he apparently got dressed, then heard the clicking of the door to their room as he left it.

He still hadn't come back a half hour later after she'd packed all her things and walked away from The Little Love Nest for good.

11

FOR THE NEXT six weeks, Pamela threw herself whole-
heartedly into her job. The teens at the center probably
would have preferred that she'd wallowed at home and
left them alone, but she needed an outlet for her energy.
So she nagged. She cajoled. She counseled, listened and
tried to be a friend to some of the kids who hadn't had
an adult friend in their lifetime.

She didn't see Ken. She thought about him once in a
while—okay, constantly. But she didn't see him.

He called once, leaving her a message on her machine
telling her he'd be waiting for her when she was ready
to talk.

She wasn't ready yet. She didn't know if she would
ever be. She had recognized over the weeks that Ken
had probably been completely right in thinking she had
been all set to go out to Tahoe and get herself hurt
again. That didn't mean she'd forgiven him for deceiv-
ing her in order to help her. Nor for doing it because her
father had asked him to, though her father had told her
he didn't believe that's why Ken had gone on the trip.
He couldn't, however, offer any better explanation. So
she'd had to believe the worst for the past month and a
half.

"You going to stay here until after dark again tonight?" LaVyrle asked as she came back into the small office the two of them shared at the recreation and counseling center. "Or am I finally going to be able to get home and have dinner with my honey-pie?"

"You don't have a honey-pie," Pamela retorted.

"I do now. He's on channel eight at six-thirty and, girl, I have never seen a weatherman who can make the humidity go up so high so fast! Me 'n' Wanda have decided we need to study up on our weather-ology and then arrange a field trip for some of the kids down to the TV station. Oh, my, I think I see some cumulus clouds on my horizon." She fanned herself, rolling her eyes, obviously trying to make Pamela smile, just as she'd been trying to do for weeks.

Pamela chuckled in spite of herself. "Well, I hate to tear you away from dinner with your TV lover. You don't have to stay with me, you know. I can lock up by myself."

LaVyrle snorted. "I am not leaving you here by yourself until all hours of the night!"

"She won't be by herself." They both jerked their heads toward the door, shocked as a male voice interrupted them. "I'm here."

"We're closed, mister," LaVyrle said, putting her hands on her hips and glaring suspiciously at the intruder. "The kids have all gone home."

"Ken," Pamela whispered, knowing it was him, though he stood in the shadowed hallway outside her door. She would have known it was him even without recognizing his voice. Her whole body went on high alert, tingling with anticipation just because he stood a few feet away.

Drat the man for still being able to affect her like this!

LaVyrle looked between Pamela's face and Ken's, obviously recognizing the name. She couldn't have missed Pamela's immediate tension. "Oh, boy, I'm leaving."

"Don't go," Pamela pleaded.

"Weatherman's waiting, honey. I will see you tomorrow. Or maybe I won't. Depends on how the weather holds up around *here*, I suppose." With a stern stare at Ken, she maneuvered around him, coming chest to chest in a blatant attempt at intimidation. He held her stare, nodded his head as if to say yes, he'd gotten the message and wouldn't be hurting Pamela anymore. LaVyrle studied him for a moment, then left the room, a small smile playing about her lips. Obviously, she liked what she saw. *The traitor.*

The walls of the cramped office closed in around them with a deep, heavy silence. Pamela busied her hands, locking her desk drawers so she could leave, not even looking up at him.

"Have you talked to your father?" he finally asked.

She shrugged, knowing she didn't have to answer yet wanting to anyway. Just so he didn't think he intimidated her, standing there all dark and intense and gorgeous in the doorway. "Yes."

"You've made your peace?"

"I suppose so," she admitted, her tone grudging. "I've lived twenty-six years of my life ruing the fact that my father likes to sing my praises to pretty much anyone who'll listen. I guess Peter was a good listener."

"So you've forgiven him."

"For the most part."

"But not me."

She stood, grabbed her black nylon gym bag and stepped out from behind her old scarred-up metal city-issue desk. She held her head up as she walked the few steps across the room, waiting for him to move. He didn't get out of the way, merely stood there, blocking the door. Since she was nearly as tall as he, they came nose to nose. Pamela ignored the sensations *that* brought—the minty-sweet smell of his breath, the flicker of energy that passed between their bodies, held so rigidly, mere inches apart.

"Will you excuse me?" she finally managed to bite out. "I'm ready to go home now."

He muttered something under his breath, something that sounded suspiciously like "stubborn as a mule," but finally stepped aside to let her pass. She flipped off the light switch as she left the office, leaving him standing in the darkness. "Are you going to come out or am I supposed to lock you in there for the night?"

He finally exited, watching while she locked the office door and dropped her bulky key ring into her bag.

"Can we go have dinner somewhere, just to talk?"

"I'm not hungry," she said as she turned away and marched purposefully down the hall toward the building's exit. He followed, of course. When they reached the gymnasium, she entered the double doors to ensure the overhead lights had been turned off. They had.

Ken stepped in behind her, again blocking her path when she turned to leave. His nearness was disconcerting, distracting. Devastating.

She hadn't forgotten, in the six weeks since she'd seen him, just how strong the physical attraction had been between them. She'd never experienced anything like it before. She doubted she ever would again.

"Please, Pamela. Let's go somewhere and talk. I've missed you so much," he said, raising his hand to brush his fingers against her cheek.

"I said I'm not hungry," she finally managed to say, her words ending in a near croak as he stepped closer. She took a tiny step back. "Now, I have to go. Goodnight, Ken."

He muttered something again, then said, "Play me."

She paused. "What?"

"Play me, Pam, for talking points. Isn't that what you call them? Come on. You scared?"

"Of you? Get real, McBain, you computer-obsessed couch potato. I would whip your ass all over the court."

He chuckled. "So put your money where your slam dunk is. Play me. For every point I score, you listen to me—*really* listen."

"And for every point I score?"

He paused, considering. "I'll listen to you."

"Nope," she said with a snort. "I don't have anything to say to you." She tried to push past him and exit the darkly shadowed, cavernous room.

He caught her arm. "Wait a minute,"

"Have you got something better to put on the table?"

she asked, cocking her head to one side and putting her fist on her hip in an unspoken challenge.

He glanced around, as if searching for an answer in the silent, sweat-tinged air of the gym. Then he grinned. "Maybe. How about cash? For every point you score on me I'll donate a thousand dollars to the center. Win or lose, a thousand bucks a point. What do you say?"

Her mouth dropped open.

"We'll play single point one-on-one," he cajoled.

"To eleven or twenty-one?" she asked, still not quite believing he was willing to spend thousands of dollars just to get her to listen to him.

"Twenty-one. I have a feeling it's going to take until at least twenty for you to admit you love me."

She snorted at his arrogance, then threw her gym bag on the floor. Shaking her head, not quite believing she was going to do this, she flipped on all the light switches lining the wall by the exit. The overhead fluorescent fixtures buzzed, then flashed on, bathing the room in a brilliant white, letting her see him clearly for the first time that evening.

He looked tired. His face was a shade paler than she remembered, and she noticed a frown line on his brow. The man was still devastating, of course, even dressed casually in a gray cotton T-shirt and jeans. Tight jeans.

She mentally ordered her pulse to stop pounding and hardened her heart. Grabbing a worn, dirty-orange ball from a rack on the side of the gym, she muttered, "A thousand bucks a point, McBain."

He scored the first one. She couldn't believe it, blaming herself for being caught unaware when he stole the ball and made a nice shot that barely kissed the rim as it sailed through the net. She muttered a swear word, drawing a grin from him.

"I don't work for your father."

"That's one," she said as she stole the ball, dribbled, and countered with a point of her own.

"I owe you a thousand bucks."

"I know that. You don't get to tell me. No talking unless you score."

"No *scoring,*" he said, his tone making his sexual meaning clear, "unless I talk enough to convince you I'm crazy about you, either, I guess." His frustration was evident.

He distracted her, darn it. That sexy little comment cost her another shot. He took full advantage, aimed and scored again.

"I was working on a contract for your father's company that was signed, sealed, delivered and well underway before you and I ever met. You had absolutely *nothing* to do with me getting that work. And I am *not* his employee."

"That was more than one point's worth," she said, even as she thought about his words. Her father had told her something similar, so she wasn't entirely surprised to learn that Ken did, indeed, own his own computer software consulting firm and wasn't an employee of Bradford Investments.

Then she thrust the thoughts aside and concentrated on keeping the ball out of his very quick hands. She scored three more points, but they weren't easy. He was better than she'd expected. Better than the teens she usually played with here at the center.

"You're up to four grand now," she muttered, trying to taunt him into making a mistake.

He hadn't so much as broken a sweat as he guarded her. Then he stole the ball and sunk another one from the top of the key.

"Yes, your father asked me to go with you and make sure you were okay. But that wasn't why I went. I went because I had half-fallen for you before we ever met, from the first time I saw you at his office."

She listened in spite of herself. He took advantage of her interest and scored again.

"That night on the beach just cemented something that was already growing in my heart every time I saw your picture or heard your father talk about you, Pamela. I was falling fast and hard, half-gone on you before we met. And then, that night, I wanted to protect you, to make sure no one else ever hurt you again. That's why I agreed to go with you."

She sneered. "That's all?"

"Hell, no, that's not all," he retorted as he swiped the ball out of her hand, dribbled and landed a nice lay-up. "I wanted you for myself, dammit. I did not want you to go out to Tahoe and hook up with some loser."

Somehow, though he'd said it before, hearing it again like this, she started to believe him.

"And it didn't occur to you to be honest with me from the beginning? You couldn't just tell me you'd seen that awful cake incident?" That was on *her* point, but he didn't quibble.

"You wouldn't have given me the time of day. If you knew I'd been there, you would have refused even to speak to me on the beach, much less invite me to come along on a honeymoon with you."

She frowned. Yes, she had invited him, after all. He paused on the court, obviously hoping she was softening toward him. She took advantage and scored again. "There goes another thousand. I hope that contract with my father is a lucrative one."

"I'm finished with the job, Pamela," he replied as he snagged the ball and dribbled toward the basket. "I've been working sixteen-hour days, seven days a week, wanting to have the project finished. So you can't use that as an excuse between us now. I have nothing to gain by being here—except getting you to admit you love me. And to believe I love you."

She hesitated, her feet almost stumbling even as her heart tripped at his words.

She hadn't known he was finished. No wonder he looked so tired! Her father had told her Ken's project was scheduled to last for three months. He'd obviously completed it in much less time than that.

"My business is flexible, I can work from anywhere in the country. I want to stay here in Miami, permanently, with you."

"You said you were in love with me," she said softly, still not ready to forgive him just yet.

"So?" he asked, taking the ball and holding it behind his back. She grabbed for it, reaching around his waist, trying to knock at it with her fingertips.

She succeeded only in jerking her whole body against

his. They stood chest to chest. Panting. Lips parted and eyes wide. The intensity roared between them.

"Being in love with someone isn't the same as loving them," she finally said. "'In love' is a temporary condition brought about by cupids and round beds and sweet massage oil."

He smiled gently. "So what's love? Is it this? Is it sweaty basketball courts, a thousand bucks a point and a deserted rec center?"

She didn't answer.

"I *love* you, Pamela. I've loved you for longer than I've been *in* love with you."

She stared into his eyes, testing the truth there, seeing it, starting to believe it.

"I resisted it because reason and logic told me it couldn't happen. That I couldn't have fallen so hard, so fast. That you couldn't reciprocate. That it was a rebound romance."

He dropped the ball. She glanced down as it bounced away toward the middle of the court. Then he tilted her chin up and stared at her. "None of that matters. The truth is you're the other half of me, the part it took me thirty years to find. Now I've found you. You're my mate. I know it. And I'm willing to wait, or play basketball or donate a thousand bucks a point until you are ready to admit it, too."

She looked down, scuffed her toe against the floor. "I'm better than you are. You'll go broke."

"Quit stalling."

She smiled at the mock-threat in his voice. "I'm not stalling."

"You're cute when you're nervous."

"The last time you told me that I was afraid our plane was going to crash and I was going to die a virgin."

He shook his head and a wicked grin crossed his lips. "Oh, no, indeed. Too late for that, love."

"Thank goodness," she said with a tiny, heartfelt sigh.

She finally believed it, finally accepted it, finally took it all in. He loved her. Truly. With the forever kind of love that outlasted games or honeymoons or software projects.

"You still interested in the SUV and the two-point-five?"

His eyes glittered with satisfaction. "Only with you." She slipped her hands over his shoulders, circling his neck. "I love you, Ken McBain. And you're not crazy. It did happen. We were both fortunate enough to see it, feel it and recognize it instantly. You're the person I've been waiting for all my life."

His kiss was tender, sweet, gentle and laden with restrained passion. He held her tightly, as if he'd never get tired of holding her in his arms, and she sank against him, feeling complete again for the first time in more than a month.

Finally, when he tipped her chin with his index finger and tilted her head back for another kiss, she gave him a wicked smile. "This still doesn't let you off the hook. I believe the score is six to five," she said.

"We still playing to twenty-one?"

"Only if you tell me you love me for every one of your talking points."

"How about every other?" he asked as he scooped up the ball and took a long shot from half court. He landed it. She couldn't believe he landed it.

"Why every other?"

"Well," he replied as they walked hand in hand to the end of the court to retrieve the ball. "I figured the other half of the shots I'll be telling you everything I plan to do with you when we get back to The Little Love Nest for our *real* honeymoon."

They paused, Pamela raising her eyebrow, her heart beginning to pound. Then he beckoned her closer, gesturing with his index finger until her face was inches from his.

"Starting," he said with a sultry whisper as he nibbled on her earlobe, "with telling you why I'm so very happy you're tall."

Harlequin truly does
make any time special....
This year we are celebrating
weddings in style!

A
Walk
Down
the Aisle
WEDDING CELEBRATION

To help us celebrate, we want you to tell us how wearing the Harlequin wedding gown will make your wedding day special. As the grand prize, Harlequin will offer one lucky bride the chance to **"Walk Down the Aisle"** in the Harlequin wedding gown!

There's more...

For her honeymoon, she and her groom will spend five nights at the **Hyatt Regency Maui.** As part of this five-night honeymoon at the hotel renowned for its romantic attractions, the couple will enjoy a candlelit dinner for two in Swan Court, a sunset sail on the hotel's catamaran, and duet spa treatments.

A HYATT RESORT AND SPA

Maui • Molokai • Lanai

To enter, please write, in, 250 words or less, how wearing the Harlequin wedding gown will make your wedding day special. The entry will be judged based on its emotionally compelling nature, its originality and creativity, and its sincerity. This contest is open to Canadian and U.S. residents only and to those who are 18 years of age and older. There is no purchase necessary to enter. Void where prohibited. See further contest rules attached. Please send your entry to:

Walk Down the Aisle Contest

In Canada	In U.S.A.
P.O. Box 637	P.O. Box 9076
Fort Erie, Ontario	3010 Walden Ave.
L2A 5X3	Buffalo, NY 14269-9076

You can also enter by visiting www.eHarlequin.com
Win the Harlequin wedding gown and the vacation of a lifetime!
The deadline for entries is October 1, 2001.

HARLEQUIN®
Makes any time special ®

PHWDACONT1

1. To enter, follow directions published in the offer to which you are responding. Contest begins April 2, 2001, and ends on October 1, 2001. Method of entry may vary. Mailed entries must be postmarked by October 1, 2001, and received by October 8, 2001.

2. Contest entry may be, at times, presented via the Internet, but will be restricted solely to residents of certain geographic areas that are disclosed on the Web site. To enter via the Internet, if permissible, access the Harlequin Web site (www.eHarlequin.com) and follow the directions displayed online. Online entries must be received by 11:59 p.m. E.S.T. on October 1, 2001.

   In lieu of submitting an entry online, enter by mail by hand-printing (or typing) on an 8½" x 11" plain piece of paper, your name, address (including zip code), Contest number/name and in 250 words or fewer, why winning a Harlequin wedding dress would make your wedding day special. Mail via first-class mail to: Harlequin Walk Down the Aisle Contest 1197, (in the U.S.) P.O. Box 9076, 3010 Walden Avenue, Buffalo, NY 14269-9076, (in Canada) P.O. Box 637, Fort Erie, Ontario L2A 5X3, Canada.

   Limit one entry per person, household address and e-mail address. Online and/or mailed entries received from persons residing in geographic areas in which Internet entry is not permissible will be disqualified.

3. Contests will be judged by a panel of members of the Harlequin editorial, marketing and public relations staff based on the following criteria:

   • Originality and Creativity—50%
   • Emotionally Compelling—25%
   • Sincerity—25%

   In the event of a tie, duplicate prizes will be awarded. Decisions of the judges are final.

4. All entries become the property of Torstar Corp. and will not be returned. No responsibility is assumed for lost, late, illegible, incomplete, inaccurate, nondelivered or misdirected mail or misdirected e-mail, for technical, hardware or software failures of any kind, lost or unavailable network connections, or failed, incomplete, garbled or delayed computer transmission or any human error which may occur in the receipt or processing of the entries in this Contest.

5. Contest open only to residents of the U.S. (except Puerto Rico) and Canada, who are 18 years of age or older, and is void wherever prohibited by law; all applicable laws and regulations apply. Any litigation within the Province of Quebec respecting the conduct or organization of a publicity contest may be submitted to the Régie des alcools, des courses et des jeux for a ruling. Any litigation respecting the awarding of a prize may be submitted to the Régie des alcools, des courses et des jeux only for the purpose of helping the parties reach a settlement. Employees and immediate family members of Torstar Corp. and D. L. Blair, Inc., their affiliates, subsidiaries and all other agencies, entities and persons connected with the use, marketing or conduct of this Contest are not eligible to enter. Taxes on prizes are the sole responsibility of winners. Acceptance of any prize offered constitutes permission to use winner's name, photograph or other likeness for the purposes of advertising, trade and promotion on behalf of Torstar Corp., its affiliates and subsidiaries without further compensation to the winner, unless prohibited by law.

6. Winners will be determined no later than November 15, 2001, and will be notified by mail. Winners will be required to sign and return an Affidavit of Eligibility form within 15 days after winner notification. Noncompliance within that time period may result in disqualification and an alternative winner may be selected. Winners of trip must execute a Release of Liability prior to ticketing and must possess required travel documents (e.g. passport, photo ID) where applicable. Trip must be completed by November 2002. No substitution of prize permitted by winner. Torstar Corp. and D. L. Blair, Inc., their parents, affiliates, and subsidiaries are not responsible for errors in printing or electronic presentation of Contest, entries and/or game pieces. In the event of printing or other errors which may result in unintended prize values or duplication of prizes, all affected game pieces or entries shall be null and void. If for any reason the Internet portion of the Contest is not capable of running as planned, including infection by computer virus, bugs, tampering, unauthorized intervention, fraud, technical failures, or any other causes beyond the control of Torstar Corp. which corrupt or affect the administration, secrecy, fairness, integrity or proper conduct of the Contest, Torstar Corp. reserves the right, at its sole discretion, to disqualify any individual who tampers with the entry process and to cancel, terminate, modify or suspend the Contest or the Internet portion thereof. In the event of a dispute regarding any online entry, the entry will be deemed submitted by the authorized holder of the e-mail account submitted at the time of entry. Authorized account holder is defined as the natural person who is assigned to an e-mail address by an Internet access provider, online service provider or other organization that is responsible for arranging e-mail address for the domain associated with the submitted e-mail address. **Purchase or acceptance of a product offer does not improve your chances of winning.**

7. Prizes: (1) Grand Prize—A Harlequin wedding dress (approximate retail value: $3,500) and a 5-night/6-day honeymoon trip to Maui, HI, including round-trip air transportation provided by Maui Visitors Bureau from Los Angeles International Airport (winner is responsible for transportation to and from Los Angeles International Airport) and a Harlequin Romance Package, including hotel accomodations (double occupancy) at the Hyatt Regency Maui Resort and Spa, dinner for (2) two at Swan Court, a sunset sail on Kiele V and a spa treatment for the winner (approximate retail value: $4,000); (5) Five runner-up prizes of a $1000 gift certificate to selected retail outlets to be determined by Sponsor (retail value $1000 ea.). Prizes consist of only those items listed as part of the prize. Limit one prize per person. All prizes are valued in U.S. currency.

8. For a list of winners (available after December 17, 2001) send a self-addressed, stamped envelope to: Harlequin Walk Down Aisle Contest 1197 Winners, P.O. Box 4200 Blair, NE 68009-4200 or you may access the www.eHarlequin.com Web site through January 15, 2002.

Contest sponsored by Torstar Corp., P.O. Box 9042, Buffalo, NY 14269-9042, U.S.A.

PHWDACONT2

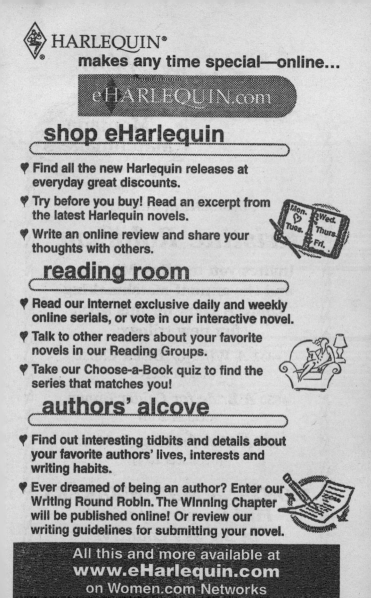